ALIEN'S TEMPTATION

Earth Brides & Alien Warriors

TINA MOSS

This book is a work of fiction. Names, characters, places, and incidents either are products of the author's imagination or are used fictitiously. Any resemblance to actual events or locales or persons, living or dead, is entirely coincidental and not intended by the author.

ALIEN'S TEMPTATION
Earth Brides & Alien Warriors, Book 3

TINA MOSS
www.tinamoss.com

Cover Design by MiblArt. All stock photos licensed appropriately.

For information on subsidiary rights, please contact the publisher at info@tinamoss.com.

2nd Edition. Originally published by City Owl Press.

Print Edition ISBN: 978-1-964370-05-7

Digital Edition ISBN: 978-1-964370-04-0

Printed in the United States of America

PRAISE FOR TINA MOSS

"*Alien's Captive* delivers steam, danger, and purpose. Filled with enticing world-building and polarizing secondary characters, it's a simple yet tumultuous introduction to this alien sci-fi romance series… Readers who love sexy aliens, death matches, and brave heroines should bypass all checkpoints to book immediate passage on this space adventure!"
— *InD'tale*

"Moss' *Code Black*, a near-future tale of paranormal humans living under the repressive Northern American United Government, chugs steadily along with occasional fireworks… A cast of vampires, psychics, and shape-shifters delivers…witty quips that round out this solid example of the genre."
— *Publishers Weekly*

"*Red Alert* is a superb read for paranormal fans. It is captivating from the first scene, and the fast pacing keeps the reader engaged for the entirety of the novel."
— *InD'tale*

"The introduction to the *Paranormal Crimes Division (PCD)* promises to be entertaining and tense. Humor is never far from the surface, which comes in handy because the world they patrol is treacherous and fear-inducing."
— *RT Book Reviews*

To the spicy seekers, whenever I think I've found the limit to how much heat I can cram between the pages, I'm wrong. Prepare for the spice. Seriously, this is your only warning. It's a plethora of alien…pickles.

Author's Note

I cannot thank you enough for picking up this book. I want you to feel safe and secure when reading. As such, I've included a list of content information available on my website at: www.tinamoss.com/content-info/

If you have any concerns about the contents of this book, please be sure to check that page first. Thank you again and happy reading!

Jane

I PACED THE CORRIDOR OF THE LANDING BAY. AS THE captain of Earth's moonbase, the heavy burden of leadership laid on my shoulders. It was foolish to volunteer for this away mission and ask my first officer to bear the weight of command in my absence. Yet, I refused to send anyone else. I'd not dare put another in danger—and not with *that* alien.

"You know you're going to wear a hole in the floor, Captain." My first officer, Mai Sato, stood with her back to the wall—out of my walking path—and held a holo-pad in front of her. Her thick bangs fell over her forehead, but I was sure it was scrunched in thought as she tapped the screen. "I've put together a list of personnel shifts for your approval and uploaded the Rhonars' information regarding the Meta Sector to your personal device."

I halted mid-step and turned toward her. Holding out my hand wordlessly for the holo-pad, I waited until she looked up at me. "You know, Mai," I took it from her, signed the bottom without reading the list, and handed it back to her, "I'm not going to be in charge in the next ten minutes. You are." I kept her gaze locked with mine and squeezed her shoulder. "And I trust you completely. Have faith in yourself."

A small smile tilted her lips at the corners. "Yes, Captain."

"And thank you for the Meta Sector information." I tapped my holo-watch on my wrist and projected the files. I swiped through the folders, noting the names for later. "Does this include the details on the ergamite crystals we need for Earth's defense system?"

"It does." She tucked her holo-pad under her arm.

"Good." I closed the projections. The ergamite was the reason I was stuck in the landing bay, waiting for the arrival of the alien warriors and my sister. Sage, second in line of us Kadaran sisters after me, was an engineer on the moonbase. But after an attack on the satellite station, she was propelled into space.

Even now, the memory of that day was enough to send me into a cold sweat. I'd never been so scared in my life. Although losing people was inevitable in a field as dangerous as ours, the thought of one of them being my sister gutted me.

She's okay. She's on her way here. I clenched my fists at my sides in the present.

Thankfully, she'd been rescued by a Rhonar warrior, and through a bizarre series of events that I was still trying to wrap my head around, she ended up mated to him. We'd held their wedding in secret to avoid tensions between the aliens and us as negotiations between our species were…complicated. My younger sisters were already planning a larger second ceremony and party when a deal was finalized between our kinds.

And that's where the ergamite came into play.

Earth's government, the Global Alliance of Nations, would agree to allow the Rhonar to seek brides from our population, if, and only if, the alien warriors proved they could protect Earth. The ergamite allowed us to create and power a defense system, according to the aliens' shared technology, which would effectively surround the planet. The system, along with continued Rhonar presence in Earth's orbit, were non-negotiable terms.

And it will protect Sage. As much as I wanted to believe I was doing this for the good of our planet, my heart knew the truth. I'd do anything for my sisters, even change the laws of the universe to see them happy. *If the big lug is who she wants, then so be it.*

At that thought, the ship carrying said big lug, my sister, and an alien that I *really* didn't want to see again touched down in the landing bay. "Chin up, Jane," I muttered and readjusted my uniform jacket. "You do not let that bastard get under your skin again."

Mai graciously kept silent at my decree.

The Rhonar space fighter was a sleek triangular shape with a silver sheen to the metal and equipped with stealth shielding. Ships just like it patrolled our orbit in intricate flight patterns. I'd be lying if I said I didn't admire the design.

As the ship landed, Mai and I stepped forward to greet its occupants. But when the hatch opened, shouts from behind us caught our attention. "Wait! Wait!" Taylor, tech specialist aboard the station and Sage's best friend, came running. Both arms loaded down with bags, she dropped them when she reached us and sucked in fast breaths. "Whoa. I am not cut out for sprinting."

"Maybe not." Mai smiled at the shorter, curvier woman. "You're built more for strength than speed."

Taylor straightened, her pale skin flushing which made her freckles stand out, and her blond hair flipping back in its ponytail. She flexed her bicep and patted the muscle. "You know it."

Before I could respond, a short brunette with wide green eyes launched from the ship. "Taylor! Jane!"

"Hey peanut." I wrapped my sister up in a bear hug and swung her off her feet. No one who saw Sage and I together would ever guess we were siblings. Adopted by the world's greatest mom, and not being blood relations, we were polar opposites in appearance. I was tall and tan with blue eyes, a wide nose, and out-of-control hair, which my mother said was a blessing of my Polynesian heritage. I tended to disagree. Sage was short and fair with green eyes, a cute, pert nose, and easy to tame locks, which I envied.

Sage laughed, the corners of her eyes crinkling. "You haven't called me that in forever." Her head cocked to the side and her smile dropped. "You worried?"

"Me?" I let my shock coat the question. "Never."

"That's a lie." Taylor piped in, taking her turn for a hug, and whispering something in my sister's ear. "The captain has been beside herself since you've been," she cleared her throat, emphasizing her words, "away."

"Well now, it's you going away, sis." Sage popped me lightly in the shoulder and waved at Mai. "You ready to be in charge, Acting Captain Sato?"

Mai's brows rose to her hair line as she clutched the holo-pad to her chest. "Ah yes, Lieutenant."

"She'll be fine." I grabbed Sage's arm and brought her attention back to me. I couldn't keep the excitement from my voice as I asked, "Now, is this the ship for the mission?"

"It is *my* ship." A hulking alien warrior emerged from the hatch. His black hair streaked with silver was tied tight at the nape of his neck. Since he had to be at least seven-feet tall, I had to crane my neck to peer up at him. My jaw clenched at that fact. His purple rimmed gray eyes bore into mine. I kept my chin raised, refusing to glance again at his chiseled chest covered only by a black vest or his thick thighs clad in leather. The tattoos on his shoulders and biceps were metallic in nature, and as I'd learned from Sage, symbolized his family and his brathers. When mated, they'd flow to his forearms and wrists in a chosen pattern for his beloved as was the way of the Rhonar. Commander Torian's arms were noticeably bare—not that I was looking.

"Sister," the warrior behind him, who I liked infinitely better, walked around the sullen commander and held his arm out to me, "it is my honor to see you again."

Clasping Brok's forearm in their warrior's grip, I smiled up at my brother-in-law. "It's good to see you too. Have you been taking care of my sister?" It was a rhetorical question. Sage had called me almost every day while aboard the Rhonar ship to spill the details about her alien husband. I'd never heard someone more in love.

Brok's face grew solemn. "I will always do so." He clasped his fist to his sternum and bowed his head. "You have my word."

I placed a gentle hand over his where it rested above his double hearts. "I know, Brok. Thank you."

Out of the corner of my eye, I saw the Rhonar commander stiffen. His gaze narrowed at my hand on Brok, as if he wanted to chop it off. I pulled away as he barked, "No more delays. We need to leave."

"Already?" Sage turned her puppy dog eyes my way, and then to her mate.

"Commander," Brok tucked her under his arm and pulled her to his side, "could we not stay a few spans? Sage has been away from the Terran's moonbase for some time, and I'm sure she'd like to catch up with everyone."

Commander Torian crossed his arms over his massive chest. His booted feet stood wide. "And that is why you've been granted time off." A ghost of a smile appeared on his lush lips but disappeared so quickly, I thought I had to have imagined it. "We have not told the Terran government about your mating yet. And you must be careful not to reveal it while you're here beyond this present company. But their government has granted you a special dispensation." He handed Brok a com-storage that he pulled from his vest pocket. "Sage spent time with us, and now you will remain on the moonbase as part of our personnel exchange to better learn each other's cultures." The commander patted my brother-in-law's shoulder. "That is until I've returned from my mission."

"Our mission," I corrected quickly. *Give this alien an inch and forget a mile, he'll take the whole damn universe.*

Commander Torian dropped his grip on Brok and angled that steely gaze of his on me. "Yes, little captain, *our* mission."

I bristled. "It's Captain, or Jane, if you can be civil enough to treat me with the respect due to me."

A light emanated from his pupils turning the gray of his eyes to sparkling silver. That ghost of a smile slipped out too. "As you wish, *Captain*." He emphasized my title in a manner that set my blood on fire—whether from anger or…something else, I didn't yet know or want to think about at all. "As we'll be partners in this mission, you may call me, Tor."

"All right, then, *Tor*." I accentuated his name as he had with my title. Choosing to be the bigger person, I stuck out my arm. Distantly, I noted that my crew and brother-in-law were watching our exchange. I had to keep pace with the cocky commander. "So be it."

He stalked toward me, and I resisted squirming by a fraction. His gaze was intense—a predator staring down prey. But I was not so easily hunted. He'd learn not to underestimate me. I swore it. When my arm was within his reach, he grabbed my outstretched fingers instead of my forearm and brought my hand to his mouth. Slowly, he kissed each knuckle, my insides heating with the intimate touch.

I gasped and whispered, "What are you—"

Before I could get my bearings, he released me and stepped back. Spinning on his heel, he headed for the ship. "Hurry along then, little captain."

Flames leapt from my ears. They must have as the fire roaring inside me needed to escape. My cheeks were hotter than the sun. "You arrogant son of a—"

Taylor sprang up in front of me, the bags she'd been carrying earlier back in her arms. "Here! Look! I packed all the necessities." She transferred the bags to me, not giving me the time to properly unleash my fury. Sage came up on my right side and Mai on my left.

"I'm going to miss you so much." Sage wrapped her arms around the bags and me.

Mai waved the holo-pad like a flag. "Don't worry, Captain. I'll take good care of the base."

Releasing me, Sage sprang behind me with Taylor at her side. Each of them laid a hand on my back and pushed me forward. "Now, be careful, sis. And com when you can."

"No stress, Cap. We've got things covered," Taylor chimed in.

The infuriating alien stood at the top of the ship's platform with a smug expression on his face. I couldn't wait to wipe it off.

"Try not to kill him," Sage whispered in my ear.

I dropped my bags and tugged them each to my side, a one-armed hug for Sage and her partner-in-crime. "I know what you two are doing." I eyed my sister. "And I make no promises."

Taylor ducked under my arm to talk across me to Sage. "You want the under or the over."

"Oh, definitely the over." Sage squinted over my shoulder at the commander. "My sister's tough. I give it a week."

The chuckles from them both had me shoving them away. I gave them each a pointed stare. "I don't even want to know."

Taylor smothered another laugh behind her hand. "I'll say five days."

"Bet," Sage said, shooting a loving grin in the direction of her hubs. "Then again, it might be less."

"No, no." A wagging finger from Taylor shot in the air. "A bet is a bet."

I picked up the bags and pointedly turned away from them. "I'm leaving now."

"Have a safe trip, Captain!" Mai called from the sidelines.

"Bye, Cap." Taylor waggled her eyebrows at me. "Be safe in all ways."

Sage slapped her arm. "You're bad." Waving a hand at me, she motioned toward the ship. "I can't hug you again or I'll start crying. So, get going and come back to us."

"Of course." I nodded and draped an arm around her one last time, despite her protests. I whispered to her, "Love you."

I felt a single tear against my neck before she swiped the rest away. "Love you too."

With no more to say, I picked up the bags that weighed a ton. *What the heck did Taylor pack in here?* I trekked up the ship's platform and through the lower hatch.

The commander waited with his arms crossed, a knee bent and one booted foot against the wall. He shot me a withering look. "Ready now?" He eyed my bags.

I hitched them higher in my arms. "Yes."

For a moment his arms extended as if he were going to take the bags from me, then he balled his hands into fists and whirled away. "Then, let's go."

"Fine by me." I rolled my eyes. Chivalry had died a long time ago on Earth, and that was when our population wasn't ninety-percent female. I didn't need anyone to save me, let alone some cranky alien.

"Hurry it up," he barked. His long legs ate up the distance.

I had to take two steps for every one of his. "You know…" I tightened my grip on the bags, fighting the urge to toss them at his head. "If you're going to be an asshat, this is going to be a long trip."

He snorted as he led the way to the bridge. Well, it was more like a cockpit with just two seats and a screen. But the panel in front housed a wide variety of controls that I was itching to learn. "Sit there," he pointed to the co-pilot's chair, "strap in, and don't touch anything."

"Might I remind you, I *am* a captain." I dropped the bags into a storage compartment and plopped in the chair.

He strapped into the pilot's seat and swept his hands over the console. "And might *I* remind *you* that I am in charge of this mission."

"What gave you that idea?" A deep, sardonic laugh bubbled from my chest. "This is a joint mission. Technically, the first between our species." I placed my fists above the control panel, daring him to say something. "We're equals."

His eyes shot daggers at me. "And do you know how to fly this ship, little captain?"

I flicked my gaze to his hands, then to the controls, and back again. "Not yet. But give me a few hours, and I will."

"Will you now?" The big jerk began the takeoff sequence with rapid movements.

I rose to his challenge, watching every move. No matter if a flipping meteor struck us, the Versaken attacked us, or a star imploded next to us, I was not taking my eyes off the controls. "Yes," I hissed between my teeth, "I will."

Tor

I WAS CREXED. WELL, AND TRULY, CREXED. TAKING THIS mission had been a fool's errand. Yet, the beat she volunteered, I could allow no other to go. The female had more courage and passion than was good for her. I'd subject none of my warriors to her wicked tongue and savage wit. No other Rhonar would be allowed to spar with her, push her, or test her. She'd drive any male to his limit. I was the commander; this was my responsibility.

And she was my mate.

Drav it all to the void! My fingers flew over the controls, the movements a reflection of my swirling emotions. For more rotations than memory, I'd been lost to the void— the biological curse of all Rhonar warriors. With our females taken from us after an attack by our mortal enemy, the Versaken, we'd been lost. Our males experienced two phases, the hunger and the void, which wiped out our emotions, leaving only suffering. A mate was the only way to regain emotions and become whole. With the discovery of the Terrans and the likelihood of their distant relations to us as one of our lost colonies, we had hope once more. Two of my warriors had found their fated mates.

I was the third.

You have no right to claim a Truxoria. I chided the happiness that bubbled within me. Without an appropriate treaty with Earth, the mated Rhonar would never be allowed to explore their bonds. And others would be barred from ever finding their mates. I was the leader of my people, the commander entrusted with our survival. If I did not succeed and provide my warriors with hope, then I would suffer with them.

I would not claim her. *Jane.*

I mentally slapped myself, my back teeth grinding. *Do not say her name, nor even think it.* My gaze locked on the screen. I had to resist temptation, no matter the cost. No one knew of the bond that called to me, begging me to become whole. I had not even told my second-in-command and best friend, Galagar, for fear he'd not approve of my decision. It was a lie of omission, and it did not sit well with me. But it had to be done.

I could no more let him know than the little captain. If she discovered we were fated mates? Well, the rebellion on Craxon would look like a celebration compared to what she might do. *Although the challenge might be fun.*

I ground my teeth harder, the accompanying crack inevitable.

Her scent clogged my nose, an enticing mix of sweetness and the wild seas of my home world. It drove me mad with longing. The desire for her collided with the call of the mate bond. My twin hearts beat hard in my chest. *I am a warrior. Trained, honed, and disciplined. I will not succumb.*

"I don't mind the silence," she said, her voice cutting into my resolve as sharp and deadly as the daggers hidden in my vest.

"Then, why break it?" I hissed. My words were harsher than I intended, but the emotional storm within me would not abate. The more I fought it, the wilder it grew.

She sighed and the sound sliced my chest. "Look, you don't like me. I get it." Her long, slender fingers came into view beside mine on the control panel. "But we need a truce, or this is going to be a very long mission."

I didn't disagree with her, but giving up this armor of indifference and arrogance risked too much. I'd not allow it. "It will be shorter without your nagging."

Her sharp inhale gutted me. "Wow. You're an even bigger asshole than I thought."

"You have no idea," I muttered under my breath. The winds inside me grew to a fever pitch, ravaging my soul.

I'd need to call a florin soon and temper the storm, or I'd be useless to do my duty. The empathetic beings were our most trusted allies. Helping us with their gifts by filling us with emotions when we had none, one of their kind could aid in controlling this windstorm of feeling within me now. In return, the florin siphoned a small amount of energy from us that they needed to live. It was a symbiotic relationship, and without them, the Rhonar would not have survived. They could not replace the need for our mates, but they could slow our downfall.

With the coordinates laid in and little else to do but stare at the emptiness of space through the screen, I toyed with summoning a florin now. I caught a brief glimpse of the source of my torment in my peripheral vision. I needed the florin's help, but I dreaded explaining the reasoning to my partner. Ire rising within me, I sucked on my tongue to keep it still.

The silence reigned between the Terran captain and me.

"Do you have any open space on this vessel?" Her question, breaking the silence, flowed over me like liquid fire.

I stomped on my growing desires, dousing them with icy words. "Does this look like a pleasure cruiser?"

"Enough." Rising from the co-pilot's chair with jerky movements, her sudden action after so much inaction drew my gaze. I needed to keep my eyes off her, but I found I could not look away. She spread her legs apart and placed her hands on her hips, staring daggers at me. Her body radiated tension. "If you're going to be such a bastard, then we might as well do something about it."

Now she had my full attention. "And what is it you'd like to do little captain?"

Her nostrils flared. If she'd had the ability of the ancient dragons from our shared myths, I'd have bet fire would have shot from them. "I'd like to knock you right on your arrogant ass!" A fist shook in my face, her slender wrist and fingers unlikely to do damage.

I laughed and rose from my seat, intentionally towering over her. "What makes you think you could, little captain?"

She snorted. "You underestimate me." The smile that stretched across her face was not friendly. "You wouldn't be the first to make that mistake."

I suspect not. This Terran was not a weak creature, but I was a Rhonar warrior. The top of her head missed the height of my shoulder by a hair. The muscles in her arms were feminine but defined. Her eyes were keen and sharp. Yet, I outweighed her by a wide margin, and I'd been in battle far longer. She was brave but outmatched. "You wish to put it to the test then?"

Her blue eyes, as bright as the crystals of the Valar caverns, sparkled. "That's the idea."

I gave her a once over, purposefully letting my heated gaze linger on her body. Her uniform jacket was navy with silver buttons, the insignia of her military inscribed on the left breast. Patches, no doubt denoting her rank, laid below. Her pants consisted of the same material. It appeared heavy and cumbersome, unfitting for warfare. Her boots were the only piece of her outfit of which I approved. Thick-soled and well-worn, she must have had them for many orbits.

"So," she tapped her chin, drawing my attention to her face once more, "do you have space for a sparring match or not?"

My jaw ticked. This female had the heart of a ljona, a native creature to our home world. The savage beast had a mane of red fire instead of fur. Hot to the touch, it could burn a warrior with a simple brush of its paw. The captain may not possess the flames, but her temperament was as fiery as the animal's hide. "Yes, little captain, I believe we have a space that can accommodate your needs."

"Great," she waved a dismissive hand at me, "then, lead the way."

I crossed my arms over my chest, not moving from my spot at the helm. Jutting my chin toward her, I said, "You expect to fight in that?"

Her brows rose to her hairline. She yanked on the bottom of her jacket. "I don't need to change a damn thing to beat you. But…" Taking one shiny silver button at a time between her fingers, she pushed each through the corresponding hole. The action revealed more of her skin and the garments underneath. When she'd had all undone, she opened her jacket to divulge a white sleeveless shirt. It clung to her body, revealing every curve.

I clenched my jaw so tight I feared my teeth would crack…again.

"I'd rather be comfortable when I kick your ass." Dropping her uniform jacket into the co-pilot's chair, she stalked forward. "Any more excuses?"

I ignored her question and stepped to the storage locker to retrieve her bags. I'd wanted to carry them for her earlier, and that thought had been enough to stop me. Showing her kindness would chip at the barrier I'd erected between us, an action I could not allow. Now, I simply grabbed the bags to save time. "I'll show you to your quarters." I walked to the back of the bridge, bags in tow, not checking to see if she followed. "Then, we may continue to the mat."

"Perfect," she said, a step behind me.

The space fighter did not have the same luxuries as our deep space or battle cruisers, but it had everything a warrior needed. My ship was comprised of two quarters for sleeping, the bridge, the engine compartment, a small mess hall with space for up to three, and the holo-room. The last was the most vital part of the vessel. Utilizing holographic technology, it allowed us to create whatever we needed to train, strategize, practice, or even relax. From artificial environments to battle scenarios, the holo-room provided it.

Now, it would present the perfect place to indulge the little captain in her request. My blood heated at the thought.

I have to call a florin. The need was rising to a crescendo. I worried that sparring with the tempting female would undo me. Spying the door to her quarters, I stopped and transferred her bags to one arm. I slapped my palm to the console and the door slid into the wall. "These are your quarters." I motioned to the open doorway with my free hand. "Do you wish to change or rest first?"

She passed me as she entered and quirked a brow. "Stalling, are we?"

I dropped her bags by the door, not daring to look at the bed. Built for a Rhonar warrior, she'd have more than enough room in it. Plenty for another to lay beside her and hold her while she slept. *Crex!* I had to get the void out of there before I exploded. "I'll give you time to settle, then we'll meet." I turned from her before I could do something foolish, like throw her on the bed and mate her. Over my shoulder, I added, "If you need food, it is one door down. Two doors is the holo-room. We'll meet there in one span."

"So, you *are* stalling." Her laughter tinkled over me as light as rain.

I huffed. "I am giving you a chance, female." I would not look at her again. I would not. My body spun despite my resolve. I captured her gaze with mine. "You'd best use the time to prepare."

"Oh, I have no fear, cocky commander." She flopped on the bed, her body bouncing once before she sunk into the softness. She sighed. "Ah, that's nice."

Crex. Crex. I didn't dare another word. Spinning on my heel, I ducked from the room and put my palm to the console. The door slid shut with a decisive swoosh. I heard her surprised mumbling from inside, but I didn't stick around to decipher it. I headed straight for my quarters on the opposite side of the hall.

With fast steps, I entered my room and shut the door behind me. Lust burned my skin and thickened my blood, hotter and denser than Syconian oil. Not even a florin could help me in this state. Only one thing might temper the edge of these desires. *But it's not what I need.*

It wasn't by a wide margin. What I required was to sink into my mate's sweet embrace and bury my cock deep inside her. Since that wasn't possible, I had to settle for a lesser option. Shedding my vest with my daggers inside, I placed it on the chest of drawers inlaid in the wall. Then, I chucked my boots and stripped off my pants. Heading for the shower, I stood under the black tiles and cranked the nozzle. The cleaning gel sprayed from the faucet, dousing me in the thick substance.

I palmed my cock. *Drav it.* The instant my hand made contact with my skin, it burned. Yet, the gel beneath my fingers provided a cooling sensation. I used it to run up and down the length of my shaft. Closing my eyes, I pictured the captain's face: her deep blue eyes, her high cheekbones, her lush lips. I imagined her beside me, long, slender fingers wrapped around my cock. Her wild hair brushed my skin.

I groaned as my touch became hers in my head. Holding my free hand against the wall, I increased the pace. My lust was too raw, too close to the edge.

"Jane," I called her name to the emptiness and let go. The black tiles ran with my desires before washing away under the cleansing gel. A blast of warm foam hit me next, dissolving the gel. My body went slack as it was cleaned and dried. I fell to my knees in the shower stall.

Shame hit me like a blow to the gut. I'd never wrestled with the emotion before, and its pungency left me raw and sick. It wasn't my lust that caused the guilt, but the fact that I'd used her, Jane, my little captain, without her consent. Even if it were only in my mind, I had used her.

I am undeserving of a mate. The clawing, biting sensations ripped at my insides.

Staggering to my feet, I stepped from the cleanser and to the wall unit that stored clothes. I donned a fresh pair of simple, loose-fitting pants. Clothed and cursed with a whirlwind of feelings, I sat on the edge of the bed. With my lust momentarily quieted, I shouted for a florin.

The empathic creature popped into the room within a beat of my call. Emerald fur appeared in my peripheral vision as it bounced around to stand before me. With a white stomach, white front paws, and a white line down its face, the surrounding emerald fur stood out in contrast. This florin had an easy communication style, sending images into my mind. Each of their kind had differing preferences from chittering vocalizations to telepathic abilities. I was thankful this one preferred the latter as the former often grated on my ears.

"Thank you for coming." I inclined my head toward the florin and remained seated on the bed. Even sitting, the florin did not stand higher than my stomach. "I have only discovered my mate a few rotations ago, and the emotions within me lack an outlet."

The florin tilted his head, sending a plethora of jumbled images to me.

"Why?" I anticipated his question. He nodded. "Well, I cannot claim her. And I have not revealed the call of the mate bond to my warriors."

He showed me a picture of two florins together, happiness radiating from them like sunshine.

"I know the value of a mate, my friend." I sighed. A depth of despair gripped me, and I struggled against the temptation to fall into it. The sensation was eerily familiar to the call of the void. "It is that I am unworthy of her. My warriors depend on me for the promise of mates. I cannot claim my own, when I have not provided them the chance for theirs."

The tiny creature hopped on his hind legs, three tails propelling him onto the bed beside me. His paws flapped rapidly. His projections showed florins working together in various tasks. Then, a warmth glided over and through me. The storms inside began to settle into calming winds, still present, but far less turbulent.

I patted his paw. "Thank you. I am in your debt."

He stretched his tiny hand toward me. I bent at the waist so he could touch my temple. A small amount of energy drained from me, no more than what I'd use for the most menial tasks. When he finished, he gave me a bow and a smile that pulled his lips into an impossible shape, and then popped from my dimension.

It was only a matter of time before the tempest roared again, but I'd take the gentled winds for as long as they lasted. I only begged Celestia that the storm within me would stay quiet until this mission was complete.

For both my sake and my unclaimed mate.

Universe help us both, if it didn't.

3

Jane

WHAT AN ARROGANT, RUDE, AND INSUFFERABLE JACKASS. The commander turned out to be an even bigger jerk than I'd first thought. I had no idea what his problem was with me, but I'd be damned if I'd let him treat me like space dust anymore. If he wanted a fight, then he was going to get one. He might be an attractive son of a viper with his black and silver-streaked hair, purple-rimmed gray eyes, square jaw, and bronzed body ripped straight from the holo-pages of a romance novel. But he was a nasty bastard who desperately needed an attitude adjustment.

And I was just the woman to give it to him.

Hopping from the bed, I used the surge of anger to prepare. I did a round of jumping jacks, squats, and push-ups to get my blood pumping. It had been a teeny bit since I'd actively trained for hand-to-hand combat. We prepped regularly on the moonbase, of course, for emergency situations. But as captain, I focused on battle scenarios, space warfare, and tactical strategies. The likelihood of my team or I facing off one-on-one with an opponent was slim…or so we'd thought. After the Versaken attack we learned anything was possible.

An error I'll soon rectify after this mission. I imagined turning the base's gym mats into a full fighting ring. I'd have everyone running daily sparring drills, even the civilians on the base. "No one will be caught unaware ever again."

With my resolve firmer than ever, I tied my hair in a tight bun at the crown of my head. I toyed with the idea of putting sharp pins in it, but I didn't believe the commander would stoop low enough to grab my hair. *All's fair in love and war.* The stray thought whispered across my psyche. I shook it free. "No, this is fine."

My uniform pants were stiffer than I'd like for a fight, but my boots were well-worn and perfect. The white tank top I typically wore under my jacket, along with a sports bra, were ideal for most physical activity. *Except the kind where clothes are a hindrance.* I snorted at that. It had been a while since I'd had *that* type of exercise. I just didn't have the same love for casual affairs as others on the moonbase. And my last relationship had been well…

"Three? No four years ago. Damn." It had been longer than I thought. My ex was a good person, but we wanted different things, and although I'd cared about her, it wasn't the deep love I craved. *Now, I sound like Kyra.* I laughed aloud in the middle of a third round of squats. At twenty-six years old, the second youngest of us Kadaran sisters was a true romantic. I was a realist, Sage was pragmatic, and the baby of the family, Daisha, for all of her twenty-three years, might be the most jaded of us all. *Stars, I miss them.*

I was lucky that Sage worked with me. With only eighteen months between us, we had always gotten along. But I was still the eldest, the born leader as they liked to tease, and I didn't like my baby sisters being back on Earth and so far from me. Even if they were full grown adults. "If all goes well with this mission, then I'll see them soon for Sage's second wedding."

I smiled at the idea. Sage might be the practical type, but she deserved her dream wedding. *I'll make it possible. I promise.*

The silent vow spurred me on. I completed my circuits, a sheen of sweat beading on my chest and forehead. Rifling through the bags Taylor had packed for me, I spotted a hand towel and used it to swipe the moisture from my skin. "Jeez, Tay, what did you put in here?"

The necessary supplies like shirts, pants, bras, and panties of various assortments were a given. The majority of them were from my wardrobe, which was standard issued military garbs. But then, I'd spotted an array of lingerie like pieces: flimsy nighties, see-through bras, and... "Is that an edible thong?"

I was going to put that tricky computer nerd on garbage duty for a month. *What was she thinking?*

I sighed at her antics and continued the search. "At least she remembered some useful things." I spotted toiletries, a holo-pad, and three packs of my favorite snack—chewy chocolate dehydrated cookies. "Okay, maybe two weeks on trash rotation."

I stared at the holo-watch on my wrist. About an hour had passed since the commander left the room. He'd said we'd meet in a span. Since I had no idea how long that translated to in Earth time, I estimated an hour was plenty long enough for whatever he had to do. *Why is he stalling?* I wondered idly at his behavior as I checked myself over and deemed me good to go. Placing my palm to the door as I'd seen him do previously, I held my breath. A wave of panic washed over me that the door might not open. I swallowed it down roughly. I hated being locked inside.

A rush of images pervaded my mind: a cramped closet, a subterranean room, a dark space. I shivered. The traumas of my childhood, after my parents died and before my second mother adopted me, lived in my skin. Half remembered nightmares, they snuck up on me whenever I least expected.

The door opened, and I breathed again.

Shaking my head of the errant memories and refusing to yield to their pull, I stalked down the hallway toward the holo-room. Passing the door he'd said was the food prep area, I popped my head in. The room consisted of a counter with two stools, a storage unit, and a wash bin.

Not much to write home about, so I didn't give it more than a cursory glance.

The next door was the holo-room, and it was far more impressive. Shaped like an octagon, it had emitters in each corner. The floor, ceiling, and walls possessed refractory paneling. I wasn't an expert on the technology, but neither on Earth nor the moonbase did we have anything as elaborate. "And I thought my holo-watch was cool."

"Did you want to stand there and gawk, little captain, or did you want to go in?" The big alien had no right to be as stealthy as he was. A male his size should not have been able to sneak up on me.

I struggled to keep the agitation off my face, so I didn't dare look in his direction. "Just waiting for you," I said, managing to sound nonchalant. Point for me.

"And have you prepared?" His deep voice reverberated down my spine like a strike—or a caress.

Damn it. You cannot let him get to you. Walking to the center of the room, I turned around slowly to face him. One foot behind me, I braced my weight evenly between my back and front legs. With my fists at chin height and elbows tight to my body, I readied my fighting stance. "Yes, I'm prepared to knock you on your arrogant ass."

He laughed. Not a snarky chuckle, but a genuine laugh from his gut. I didn't know who was more startled by the sound, for he cut it off after a second with wide, alarmed eyes. I imagined my expression matched his.

He shook his head as if to will away the merriment, and a dark shadow fell across his face. His stern brow dropped, his expression hardening as if composed of stone. He mirrored my stance. "Then let's begin."

I stood my ground by sheer force of will. The commander might be a cocky bastard, but he had reason to be. I was on the taller side for a human and still he towered over me, a mountain of muscle honed for battle. His chest was notably bare, no vest, no weapons to be seen. He wore only a pair of loose-fitting pants and his boots. I swallowed at all that skin on display. The metallic patterns on his arms glistened under the holo-lights.

"Training environment alpha-four." His command rang out, echoing in the the space. Then, the room shifted.

A woodland clearing replaced the octagonal walls. Bright purple leaves sprouted from gray tree bark, circling us in a wide ring. A spongy grass-like substance of a deep amber hue laid under our feet. Bright sunlight filtered from a lavender sky above. If not for the tension in the air between us, it would have been a beautiful place.

Stomping his front foot into the grass below, he said, "You're move, Captain."

The use of my title without the *little* in front of it caught me off-guard. I shifted my feet to catch my bearings and orient to the squishy ground beneath me. He waited as patient as any wild beast hunting its meal. His eyes held an intensity that bore a light from within.

I will not squirm. I won't. Worms danced in my gut. I could practically feel the imaginary bugs crawling inside. My stomach was a mess of nerves. I'd faced intimidating opponents before. But this alien warrior was on a whole other level. And I might have cooked up a meal I couldn't finish. *No, that's fear talking. And you are not a coward.*

Bracing my back leg to take 70 percent of my weight, I kept the front one loose and ready to strike. I had to find an opening, a weakness somewhere. Everyone had one, right? "I'll let you make the first move. Wouldn't want it over too quick."

Oh god, oh goddess. Where the hell did that come from? The bravado coming from my mouth did not belong to me. It was a mad woman talking.

His lips quirked. A fraction of the intensity lowered as he clearly struggled not to laugh. "So be it, little captain." A twist of his mouth and a smirk appeared on that handsome face. "Have it your way."

Whoa. When did I start thinking of him as handsome? I didn't have long to ponder as a sweep knocked my front leg out from under me. *Shit!* The lone saving grace was that I'd braced my back leg. With a phenomenal effort, I tucked my front leg into my chest and spun around. The blow knocked me almost in a full circle, so that I stood with my side to him. Had it been my back exposed, I would not have recovered.

Using the momentum of his strike, I flipped my leg over and delivered a side kick. But his speed saved him from getting a boot to the ribs. He grabbed my ankle and pulled me forward. I landed with my boot on the ground and my back to his chest. Exactly what I'd been avoiding the first time.

Not that easy. I ducked before he could grab me and rolled away from him. When I sprung to my feet, we faced each other once more.

"Not bad, Terran, but you'll not win by dodging." He stood in the fighting stance I'd taken once more, mimicking my moves.

I smiled at him, my cold smile I reserved for battle. "I didn't plan on it."

The commander baited me, and from the ease in his stance, he expected me to take it. Striking him again head on would be a fool's move.

I was not a fool.

"Did you want to just watch me, or were you actually going to do something?" I bounced side to side, forcing him to track my movements.

His smirk returned, a cool twist to his lips that matched mine. "I didn't want you to feel bad, little captain. You deserve a chance to try."

I laughed at his taunts. "Oh, silly commander…" I faked left, then slid under him. A desperate, suicidal move if ever I attempted one, but I saw only one weakness on him—a male's weakness. "I never try. I do."

Popping him with an elbow to the groin, I rolled forward through his legs as he groaned. But he didn't go down. Not even to one knee. *What are his balls made of steel?* I got to my feet quickly, not relishing a retaliation if I didn't finish him off. Aiming a kick to the same region, I didn't hesitate.

One large hand palmed my calf while the other hand cupped his balls. "That was a low blow, Captain."

I shrugged. "Anything goes in battle."

Releasing his groin, he hauled me into him and wrapped his free arm around my back. I wriggled against him; my leg still trapped in his fist as he tucked it to his side. The position was infuriating—and hot as hell. My pussy throbbed as he hitched me higher up his chest so that I stood on tiptoe with the one foot still on the ground. "Now, little captain, is that what you truly believe? Is there not a code of honor even among enemies?"

My eyes narrowed, ire rising along with a wave of lust at the contact between us. "Is that what the Versaken showed you?" My nostrils flared and my voice rose an octave higher. The emotions sweeping through me rocked me to the core. "Did they have honor when they shot my sister into space?"

A look I'd never seen before passed over the commander's face—compassion? Empathy? I didn't know. The Rhonar had no emotions, unless they were mated. That's what we'd been told. It was the sole purpose for their negotiations with Earth. They needed brides to complete their bonds and save them from their biological states of emptiness. So, why now did the commander have a brightness to his eyes and a curve to his mouth that hinted at more?

"No." The simple word was set in stone. "They lack all honor."

A heavy silence laid over us as we stood immobile. He held me tight, staring into my eyes with a thousand enigmatic thoughts whirling behind his stare. I tried to get free once more, but the motion did nothing but shift me in his grip. My spread leg set my pussy right at the level of his stomach, and I almost moaned as my escape attempts brushed my clit over his hard abs. My stiff pants created the perfect friction against all that muscle. I bit my bottom lip to stifle the sound.

Suddenly, he sniffed the air, breathing it deep into his lungs.

"What is it?" I searched his body, hoping to find a spot where I could strike him. My arms were still free so I had to attempt a blow somewhere, but the only place that would do any damage was his face. And...I just didn't want to hit him there.

"Your scent." He sucked in another breath and angled me lower. The movement sent my leg over his hip, and my pussy in direct contact with his hardened cock. "Crex. I can smell your arousal, little captain."

How did he recover so quickly? Moving his arm from my back to my ass, he pushed me into him, working me against his shaft. "Fuck!"

"Tell me you want me to stop." He slid me up and down, our pants the only barriers between us. "Tell me now."

Stop? I didn't want him to stop. My pussy throbbed like a second heartbeat. Lust swirled inside me like a hungry, living thing. I wanted to come on his cock more than I wanted to breathe. It didn't matter that he was a surly bastard. He was hot and hard, and I wanted more. "Don't stop."

4

Tor

My cock was as hard as Valkar metal. I wanted nothing more than to lay my mate in the grass below and ravage her. Her delicious scent filled my lungs, tempting me to taste its sweetness from the source. I'd spend rotations claiming her, devouring her, until she'd know nothing but me.

"Don't stop," she said again, testing my resolve. Her fingers dug into my shoulders. With her one leg trapped around my waist and the other dangling below, I had her at my mercy. Sliding her against my shaft, I ensured she felt everything beneath my pants. I paused only to grab her thigh and draw her other leg around me. Then, I backed her against a tree and ground my hips into her core.

I needed her to scream my name.

"I can't," she cried, her back bowing.

I growled in her ear. "Say it, little captain. Tell me who is going to make you come."

She moaned.

"I want to hear my name on your lips, Ijona." I thrust against her hard, my cock angling toward that pleasure spot all Terran females possessed. "Say it."

"You are." Her lip trembled as her jaw clenched. She was still fighting me.

I would have her surrender. "And what's my name?"

She cast me a mischievous smile. "Cocky commander."

I stopped, holding her still between my body and the tree. She wriggled in my grip, moving her hips to seek her relief. "Try again."

"Bastard." Her deep blue eyes, the most incredible hue, sparkled with fury.

"Not that either." I drew her up and down my cock… slowly. "Say it." I did it twice more, then stopped again. "Do it, Ijona. Give me the satisfaction." I began an easy rhythm, not the frenzied pace of earlier, to coax her into submission. A sigh resonated from her, the vibration of it working against my chest. When her body began to relax once more, the tension sinking from her, I picked up the pace. "Now."

"Yes." Her legs tightened around me. She buried her hands in my hair, pulling me closer. "Fuck!"

"Open your eyes, Jane." I would have her look at me. I'd have what was mine. "Come for me. And say it."

Her eyelids snapped open, her heated gaze on me. Celestia, she was beautiful. "Tor," she whispered, and I slammed my mouth on hers. I hadn't planned the kiss. But with my name on her lips, my need ratcheted higher. I wanted her to feel my passion, even if I could not claim her as I so wished.

Her entire body went rigid, and I pulled away from the kiss, needing to see her desire reach the peak.

"Tor!" she screamed, and it was the most incredible sound. I held her tight as she rode the waves of her orgasm. The tides crashed through her body, and she held onto me like a lifeline. I'd not leave her alone.

When the storm passed, she slumped against me, her head resting in the crook of my neck. I breathed her in, loving the feel of her breasts against my chest, her hair tickling my nose. Desire swam through me, but it had tempered a fraction with her satisfaction, as if I too received pleasure. In truth, I did. Hearing my name from my mate's lips was ecstasy. I yearned for more.

Yet, I'd dare claim none.

With the warring thoughts of desire and duty mixing within me, I held the little captain close and carried her from the holo-room. The computer flipped off the artificial environment as I exited to the hall.

"Where are we going?" The fierce Ijona asked on a yawn.

I smiled against her hair. "You need to rest."

"Bossy, alien." Her words held no heat as she snuggled into my chest.

At this rate, she'd be asleep before I made it to her quarters. Knowing the captain's resolve, she had likely spent the prior evening preparing for our mission. Tactical reports and a study of the ergamite would have kept her from her bed. *If you were truly mine, you'd never want for anything, Jane.* I took an extra few beats outside her door to relish the feel of her in my arms. *You'd have everything you desired, and I'd make sure you got your rest.* I laughed silently at the fantasy. *After you were well satisfied.*

I allowed the harmless fiction. Knowing it could not be so between us didn't stop me from wanting it to be different. I craved this Terran more than I'd wanted anything in my life. But I was bound to my brothers, and I would not abandon them.

But if the mission succeeded—

Before I could entertain that thought, an alarm blasted through the ship. "Warning. Warning. Attack incoming."

Jane's eyes popped open, her body stiffening on full alert. She jumped from my hold, landing on her feet and straightening with the skill of a honed fighter. It took me longer to process her actions than for her to take them.

"We need to get to the bridge," she said, looking me up and down. "Grab your weapons and meet me there."

I was momentarily dumbstruck as she took off.

"Enemy fire detected. Impact in one click." The ship's computer knocked sense into me and set me in motion.

Heading to my quarters, I grabbed my vest and the weapons hidden within. I didn't bother with anything else. We didn't have time, and I needed nothing more. When I arrived on the bridge, the little captain had strapped into the co-pilot's chair, and her fingers were flying over the controls. I didn't bother to ask what she thought she was doing. I'd seen her following my piloting movements earlier, like a sao-sao bird watching their nest.

"Status?" I asked, taking my seat and scanning the computer's report.

The screen flipped to the outside view, the sight unwelcoming. "Five Versaken ships." Jane motioned toward the blinking button in the middle of the console. "I've sent a message to the moonbase to warn them. But we can't give-up. We have to complete the mission."

"I have no intention of giving up." Ducking under the console, I palmed the device required to get us to our destination.

"Thirty beats to impact." The ship's countdown grew dire.

The captain set her hand over my wrist as I brought the device atop the console. "We can't use that yet. We're not at the coordinates."

I plugged the device into the ship's navigational drive and powered it on. "There's no choice. We don't have the fire power to match five Versaken vessels, nor can we use stealth shielding as their sensors already have a lock on us." My fist clutched the device, struggling not to crush it in my hand. Traveling without stealth mode was a novice mistake. I'd let my desire for the Terran distract me from my duty—as I'd feared. "And we cannot go back."

"My sister was clear about it." Jane bit her lip, indecision warring on her face. "She reconfigured the wormhole generator from the enemy's tech. And she was adamant we use it only at the designated spot." Snaking her hand away, she nodded once. "But you're right. If we don't use it now, we won't have the chance."

"Ten beats to impact."

"Then, we're agreed." I reclaimed her hand, holding it in mine. If it were to be my last moments, I'd enjoy what pleasures I was allowed. And if we survived, I'd do better to behave like a proper commander. *I must.* Setting the device to propel the wormhole directly in front of us, I hoped to prevent the Versaken ships from following.

She sucked in a breath and squeezed my hand. "Do it."

"Three...two..."

The wormhole generator interfaced with the ship and a thick spiral opened in space. Taking up the screen, its menacing swirls sucked us in.

"I hate velocity rides!" Jane yelled over the g-forces slamming us into our seat-backs.

I didn't know what a velocity ride was, but I agreed. The jaunt through the wormhole was not a journey I wished to repeat anytime soon. Between the spinning of the ship and the immense pressure, it was worse than battling a stechreton—the hard-plated beasts that roamed the swamplands of my home world. The creature attacked with teeth as big as a warrior's head, six prehensile limbs tipped with claws, and a heavily spiked tail. And yet I'd take that fight over this barbaric ride.

"Is…" Another twist of the ship rolled us upside down. "…it…" Our joined hands locked tight against the console. "…over?"

Her words were strained. I wanted to reassure her, but in truth, I had no idea when the nightmare ride would end.

Then, the ship jolted forward, flipping one last time before it came to a halt. "Transfer complete," the computer intoned. "Arrival: Meta Sector, location 321, 48, 87. Twelve parsecs from destination."

I waited a beat for my body to adjust, then cut my gaze to the captain. Her hands rested on either side of her temples, rubbing lightly.

"Oof," she tilted her chin up, pushing the back of her head into the seat-back. The circular style in which she had done her hair hit the headrest. "That was awful."

Unstrapping from the pilot's chair, I rose slowly. My stomach didn't relish the movement, but I ignored it. "Computer, scan area and run full diagnostics." Decoupling the wormhole generator from the ship, I placed it in the storage compartment under the console. Then, I turned to the little captain. "You all right?"

Her eyes were glassy and her breathing rapid. But she shot me a weak smile. "I'll live. You?"

She's concerned about me. A jolt of surprise ran through me, and I wasn't sure I was successful from keeping the emotion off my face. "Fine."

"What?" She snorted, removing her straps and stretching her limbs. "Big bad warriors don't get motion sickness, or is it just a faux pas for me to ask?"

"No, that's not—" For a second time we were interrupted by alarms.

The console lit up, and the computer said, "Incoming vessel detected bearing 330 mark 15."

"Drav it." I settled back into the pilot's chair, shifting the screen to those coordinates and directing the ship to conduct a scan of the unidentified craft. "Life signs? Weapons?"

"Thirty-two Mangox aboard." A spaceship came into view, a massive battle cruiser at least ten times our size. "Weapons active."

"Open a channel." Our space fighter was outfitted with hyperdrive and laser rays. We could choose to flee or fight, but with a ship that size, it'd be a hard choice either way. Not as dire as the Versaken situation, but not good. The Mangox were a bastard species who preyed on those weaker than themselves. They were the highest, ruling gang of scum in the Meta Sector, controlling all unsavory trade in the area from species trafficking to banned weapons procurement. I swallowed my disgust for their villainy before responding. "Mangox ship, I am Commander Torian of the Rhonar warriors."

An unsettling countenance appeared on the screen as the computer switched to communication's mode. "Ah a Rhonar." Beady eyes stared from a triangular face consisting of brown fur, a long thin snout, and short rounded ears. A beige button-down uniform shirt stretched across a barrel chest. Arms as thick as tree trunks waved at the screen in greeting. "Haven't seen your kind around these parts for a time."

"Indeed. It's been several rotations." I inclined my head a fraction to acknowledge his point without giving away anything.

The Mangox's rounded eyes grew brighter. "Rumor has it you're searching for females, specific females."

Jane gasped. I tightened my fist under the console, silently begging her not to speak.

"We are always in search of a mate." I kept the Mangox's focus on me. Although the computer projected only my image to the bastard, I didn't want him asking questions about my co-pilot if he caught wind of her. "They are sacred to all Rhonar. But tell me, friend, who am I speaking to?"

I didn't care about his name in the slightest, but the more I could steer the conversation from me—and Jane—the better.

"How rude of me. I am Capo Mulo." He swept his beefy arm around. "And what may I ask are you doing in the Meta Sector, Commander?"

"We seek passage to Sense VII." The truth was the easiest story to stick with. He didn't need to know the reason behind our visit to the planet. It was a popular destination run by a Kinsian couple for a variety of needs—and desires. A trip there would not be suspicious.

Mulo laughed, a rolling sound like a pebble in a box. "And who is we?"

"That would be me." Jane's voice reverberated through the com, but the computer would not project her image on the screen without my orders.

Crex. Can't let down my guard. I slammed my fist on the console. "My ship's occupants are of no concern of yours."

"No need for hostilities, Rhonar." The beady-eyed bastard looked over my shoulder as if he could search inside the ship. "Let us come aboard. We'll meet your crew, and then, escort you in your travels." He picked at a piece of errant dirt from between his claws. "This is a dangerous part of the galaxy after all. Wouldn't want you to come to harm."

A rush of ire ripped a path up my spine. I didn't want these crexers anywhere near Jane or the ship. But if we fought now, we risked failure. No matter the cost, we had to complete the mission. My body was rifled with tension, muscles locking and readying for battle.

"That's a kind offer, Capo." The little captain's words were laced with sweetness, but I heard the bite behind them. "But the commander and I prefer to be alone."

"Hah!" Mulo's gaze wandered the screen, searching for her. "Now, my dear, I must insist. I have to meet the holder of so lovely a voice."

"You heard her." I clenched my fists at my side, willing my hearts to slow their rapid beat. "We desire our privacy."

"Commander Torian," the capo's attention snapped back to me, "I am afraid I am not giving you a choice." His snout flared upward like a feather caught in a breeze. The mouth under his thin trunk flashed an array of small, yet wickedly sharp teeth. "As the protectors of this sector, we must know who occupies our space. We would not want ruffians causing trouble."

Protectors, my ass. I bit back the growl that lodged in my throat. *You mean you don't want a rival gang encroaching on your claimed territory.*

A feminine laugh broke the tension. "Capo Mulo, you flatter us. Do we look like ruffians?"

His head whirled around at the sound of her words, once again seeking Jane. "Now, fair one, I don't know *what* you look like." Suddenly, the video on the com cut out and only the audio projected his decree. "But I will find out. Prepare to be boarded in ten clicks."

"Transmission ended." The computer's announcement punctuated the disastrous finale to the encounter.

"Drav it!" I struck the console again. *That was worse than I anticipated.* My mind spun with options, every one of them bad.

Jane's soft hand landed on my arm. "I tried to follow your lead, but they made up their minds the moment they spotted us."

"You don't know that." I growled at her. "You should have stayed quiet."

Her hand snapped back as if burned. "We're partners on this mission. I won't remain silent when we're threatened."

"I could have handled them. They don't care about one Rhonar warrior off on a pleasure jaunt." I stalked toward her, forcing her to step back until she had nowhere to go. "But once the Mangox heard you, nothing would stop them from learning more about you. You're the reason they're boarding this ship."

She flinched as if I'd slapped her. The pain in her eyes turned my blood cold. I spoke the truth, but I didn't mean for it to hurt her. "I'm sorry," she said on a whisper. "I didn't realize."

I sighed and palmed her cheek. "I should have warned you. You don't know the dangers of life out here."

"I'll learn." A flush warmed her skin. "I'm a fast learner."

"Good." I let my hand drop, although it was the last thing I wanted to do. "You'll need to be a quick study and a damn fine actress for this next part."

One dark brow rose. "What do you mean?"

"I mean, little captain," I stepped closer, our bodies brushing, "you'll need to pretend, put on a show for these Mangox bastards."

"What kind of show?" Wariness laced her question.

"The Mangox view everything in the universe as commodities: weapons, supplies, planets, even people." I leaned in closer, my mouth at her ear. "You are magnificent, strong and brave." I captured her gaze with mine, wanting her to see the truth in my eyes. "But they will not understand that. They will see you as a prize to be bought and sold."

"You're telling me they'll want to own me?" She swallowed roughly.

"Yes, ljona. But they can't have you." I wrapped my arm around her, needing the nearness. "You are mine."

5

Jane

THE META SECTOR WAS OFFICIALLY THE MOST SCREWED up place in the universe. Not that I knew anything about space beyond the surrounding light-years of my own galaxy, but I couldn't imagine anywhere being worse than here. "So, you want me to pose as your slave?"

"Yes, little captain. If the Mangox believe I am your master, they may try to buy you, but they will not attempt to steal you." Tor rifled through my bag on the floor. We'd come to my quarters after he explained our predicament. With the bastards boarding our ship in less than ten minutes, we had to act fast. "They'd consider it bad form. Their code is not one of honor, but of commodification. They respect transactions." He pulled free one of the lingerie pieces, much to my horror, and held it up. "What of this?"

"You can't be serious. I didn't even pack that! Taylor did," I squealed, unable to keep my calm. "It's not meant to be worn in public." The two-piece nightie consisted of a royal blue halter top, matching high-cut panties, thigh highs, and a garter belt with straps.

"It will match your eyes." His smirk was hot as hell.

In other circumstances, I'd consider donning the skimpy outfit for him. Although, I wasn't sure I liked the bossy commander, my body didn't seem to have any problem with him. "I don't care. It's too revealing to wear in front of those creepy, hairy elephant assholes."

"Ljona," he said, dropping the lingerie on the bed and taking my hands in his, "I would kill them all, if it meant keeping you safe. But if I were to fall, they would take you and sell you on the dark market." He squeezed my hands. "I am but one warrior. I know you can fight, but we are outnumbered."

"We could try another wormhole trip." My stomach rebelled at the mere mention of the idea. "Or doesn't this baby have light-speed or something?"

"We have sonic speed with the hyperdrive, but making an enemy of the Mangox is not wise, if we can avoid it." Tor brushed strands of hair from my cheeks and tucked them behind my ear. "We need to complete our mission. And the Mangox own the Meta Sector. Eventually, they'd hunt us down."

I sighed. "There's no other option is there?"

"No," he growled low in his throat, the sound rumbling in his chest, "I do not relish the thought of them seeing you in such garments either."

"Commander Tor, that almost makes it seem like you care," I teased. Being a grown-ass woman of thirty-one, I did not kid myself that our sexy scene from earlier was anything more than two people working off steam. While I enjoyed the big warrior's body, since oh what a body it was, it did not mean I was ready for anything beyond that. He was still an arrogant son of a viper. It just so happened there were a helluva lot worse aliens than him in the universe.

His cocky ass smile returned, and I didn't mind it as much as before. It lit up his face and softened his harsher edges. "Do not sass your master, ljona."

"Oh, you're going to enjoy this way too much." I snagged the lingerie off the bed, already dreading this scenario. "Turn around so I can put this on before those bastards come."

He rolled his eyes in an all too human gesture but complied. "As you wish, Captain."

"Well, at least you got my title right for once." I shucked off my boots and pants quickly. If I thought too much about it, I'd chicken out. Gripping my tank top at the hem, I tugged it over my head and slapped it on the growing pile of clothes on the floor. Standing in my sports bra and boy-shorts, I lost my nerve. "Are you sure I can't just wear this?"

"I can't see what you're wearing." He remained faced away from me but pointed to his back. "Sadly, I do not have eyes here."

I huffed. "Turn around then."

He did so, and my skin flushed with heat. Those damn gray-purple eyes of his illuminated as if from an inner light. His stare was intense and burning hot. "You are a female of incomparable beauty, little captain." He stepped into my space, crowding me with his presence. "And other than having you stroll around naked, I'd prefer you in this." He stroked the waistband of my boy-shorts with featherlight caresses. "But I'm afraid your current clothes would not be believable for a slave."

Sighing, I twisted the skimpy lingerie between my hands. "Fine. I'll put it on. Turn back around."

Tor, to his credit, didn't say anything. He simply put his back to me once more and gave me the time to come to terms with our circumstances. I'd never posed as anyone's slave that was for sure. I didn't attempt role-play or BDSM scenes in the bedroom. I was an A-type through and through in every facet of my life. While others dreamed of letting go, I craved control. *Yeah, and that's not an issue, right?*

I did not need to psychoanalyze my life right now. So, I stomped on those thoughts as I pushed off my boy-shorts, flipped my sports bra over my head, and pulled up the bikini panties. It wasn't quite as bad as a thong, but my ass-cheeks still showed through the high-cut sides. I grimaced. The halter top was easy enough to manage, but the garter was something else. "Shit. This is annoying."

"May I help, little captain?" The commander stood unmoving from his position, but a low hum of tension radiated from his body.

Having no clue how to hook in the garter's suspender pieces on the stupid outfit, I admitted defeat. "Yes." I walked around him and handed him the straps. "You can help me with these."

He sucked in a breath as he stared at me, holding the suspender in a clenched fist. I had the urge to cover up. I wasn't ashamed of my body, or anything, but well, I guess I was more on the modest side. Strutting around in anything skimpier than a workout bra and shorts just wasn't my style. No hate to others who rocked it, but it wasn't for me.

"You are truly a wonder," his words hissed between his teeth. "I am unworthy of such a," he opened the suspender's snap and placed it on my garter belt around my waist, "partner."

I blinked rapidly, flutters winging in my belly. "Ah, thanks." I had no idea what to do with flattery. A cocky, arrogant commander I could handle. But one who paid me compliments and looked at me like I was the center of his orbit? No clue.

His lips pressed together in a slight grimace. Then, he appeared to gather his senses and narrowed his eyes. "Right. Let's get you settled." He knelt before me, and the air left my lungs. I didn't dare move. Palming the back of my thigh, he brought it closer to him. "Here."

He snapped the opposite end of the suspender that hung from my waist to the strap around my thigh. With one piece in place, he let my thigh go, and then he palmed the other, repeating the process. When he finished, he rose and took stock of his work. "Perfect."

"I appreciate your help," I said, proud at myself for the calm tone. My heart was beating faster than a space speeder. The silky fabric was cool against my heated skin. I had to admit it felt good, soft and lush. But as Tor's stare burned hotter than a blue star, I hated having to go and put on an act for the alien scumbags. "What do I need to expect from these Mangox?"

A dark laugh barked from him. "Nothing good." His nostrils flared, and he ran a hand through his hair. "Just call me, Master. Nothing else. And try not to argue with my orders."

I snorted. "This is going to be impossible."

He held his palms out in front of him. "Believe it or not, I understand." Tentatively, he let one hand wrap around my upper arm. "If our roles were reversed it would be hard for me to give up control too."

"It's not personal. I'd be this way with anyone." Staring at his hand on my arm, I took a single step toward him. "Although you are an arrogant ass."

"I am." He nodded and a softer smile eased the lines around his eyes. "But I'll work on it, okay?"

That fluttery sensation in my stomach returned with a vengeance. "I'll hold you to it."

"Deal." He brought me the rest of the way, hugging me to his chest. His arms around me were warm and hard, comfort and protection in one.

Okay, so, maybe I liked him a little.

TOR

My thoughts tumbled one over the other. As her cheek nuzzled my chest, my plans shifted. I'd vowed to deliver hope to my brathers. For them I would move the stars. But for her, I would collapse the cosmos. I had to complete this mission. It was the only chance I had of making Jane truly mine.

We had to succeed at any cost. That included ensuring her safety from these Mangox crexers.

"Captain." I held her by her upper arms. Her head tilted up, her eyes a bit glassy. My proud fighter was struggling with this ruse, and we hadn't yet begun. I had to aid her. "You're safe with me. I will never harm you."

"I believe you, Commander." A wary smile warmed her face, then her cheeks began to darken. "Or should I say," she swallowed roughly, "Master?"

Drav it all. I'd be lying if I denied my blood heated from that honorific spoken from her desirable mouth. I choked on the gravel in my throat. "Let's save it for the Mangox." I pushed her gently from me and tucked her arm around mine. "Ready?"

"No." She sighed but straightened and stood tall. Freeing her hair from its usual up-style, she let it flow wild and free around her shoulders. "But let's do it anyway. Brief me as we walk."

We headed toward the rear of the ship where an airlock would feed their platform to our ship and allow the bastards access. "It'll be easiest if you are yourself as much as possible, so you're not playing a character." I tapped in the sequence that bypassed security and opened access to our ship. My skin grew cold as I did so, but I focused on the little captain as a distraction. "Did you have any rigid instructors in your military training?"

She snickered at that. "Oh yeah."

"Pretend you're deferring to one of them." I narrowed my eyes at her. "You weren't a student who mouthed off, were you?"

Her chin raised, an indignant pout to her lips. "I was a model student."

"Good." I hid my smile behind my free hand. I'd imagined nothing less from a ljona. Like the creature I named her for respected pack order, my little captain understood hierarchy, especially in battle. "Pretend then, I'm one of your past instructors. Instead of calling me…?" I let my voice trail into a question.

She raised a brow at me before she understood. "Sir. We called our instructors, Sir, regardless of gender."

"Then, replace Sir with Master, and imagine I'm your teacher." I squeezed her arm before reluctantly letting go and standing stoically beside her. "You can do this, ljona."

"I know." Cocking her head to the side, she looked at me through her peripheral vision. "Why do you keep calling me, ljona? I meant to ask before, but I was, um, well," she bit her lip, "distracted."

"And what a distraction it was," I reminded her.

Her breathing sped up, but she waved her hand as if to dismiss the memory. I'd let that slide, for now. She continued, "Uh-huh. Anyway, I get the little captain reference. Not very inventive, by the way." She rolled her sea blue eyes, a gesture I enjoyed copying from the Terrans. "But ljona doesn't translate. What is it?"

"A fierce creature from my home world." The ship thumped as the Mangox vessel connected with ours. In another click they would board. "It has a fiery mane that can burn a warrior with one touch, but it is a rare and beautiful creature." I turned to capture her gaze one final time before we took on this charade. "Just like you."

The hatch opened before she could respond, and we both spun toward the door.

"Ah Commander," the seedy Capo Mulo threw his arms wide as he stepped onto the ship, "thank you for having us aboard."

The capo was flanked by three subordinates, each wearing a black uniform shirt and standing a head taller than him. Since their leader met me at eye-level, none of them could be considered small. All four Mangox were bare from the waist down, covered in thick, brown fur. They did, however, wear belts around their sizable waists, which housed com-units and blasters.

Jane shifted one foot behind her as if to take a fighting stance. Tugging her into my side, I put my arm around her shoulders to prevent the movement. If the Mangox showed any signs of attempting to steal her from me, I'd kill them all. But until then, an aggressive stance would not help our cause.

"Indeed." I didn't move, forcing them to keep their position at the rear. "As you can see, my vessel is not large enough to accommodate your party." I motioned toward the three males behind him. "It's a fighter, not a cruiser."

Mulo laughed, a barreling noise that was half-roar, half-mirth. "I understand, Rhonar. Do not fear." His blatant stare assessed me from head to foot and back again. "We don't plan to stay long." His gaze shifted to Jane, and it took all of my will not to rip his beady-eyes from his skull. "It was mere curiosity that brought us forth."

I pushed the little captain behind me, and to my infinite gratitude, she did not fight me. "Now that it's been satisfied, you may return to your vessel." I opened the airlock door to punctuate my words. "And we may continue on our way."

"We will, we will." The capo waved his meaty paw as if my actions were of no consequence. "But first I'd like to offer you top price for your female." He threw a bag that clinked as it hit the floor. It was the distinctive sound of drauma coins, the prevalent currency in the sector. "Her appearance is quite," he cocked his head, angling for a glimpse of her, "unique."

Jane stiffened behind me, her nails digging into my arm. I shared her sentiment, my blood boiling. I growled my answer. "She is not for sale."

Mulo's guards moved to either side of him, hands on their blasters. They would never have the chance to use them. "At ease." The capo waved them off with a snap of his claws. "The Rhonar and I are simply talking." His eyes narrowed as if daring me to disagree. "Are we not, Commander?"

"That depends on your intentions, Mangox." I used his species name like the curse that it was.

Another barking-roaring laugh emanated from him. "Your kind is always the same. So serious." His snout twisted side-to-side as his mouth curled upward. "I respect your property. We are not thieves. We're merchants."

That's a generous assessment. I refrained from saying otherwise, but I did not allow Jane to move from behind me. She kept thankfully quiet during the encounter.

"Come with us to our outpost." The capo drew close enough to extend his paw to me. "I'll buy you a drink, and we shall talk more about negotiating a trade."

"We can talk business all you like." I let his hand linger in the air. My power bubbled beneath the surface. Every Rhonar had a unique ability. With mine, I had but to touch an individual to discover their intentions, along with their strengths and weaknesses. Yet, I didn't need to shake this bastard's hand to know his purpose. It was written on his face. I'd not allow him to fulfill it. "But *not* for her."

He curled his claws into his hand, then his hand to his chest. "As you say, Commander." Reclaiming the bag of drauma coins, he turned to one of his underlings. "Send the coordinates to their ship. They'll follow us to the outpost, and there we will continue our discussion."

The subordinate nodded to his leader, then the crew headed for the airlock.

"But we need to go to Sense VII," my little captain yelled from behind me. With her hands on my waist, she popped her head out to sneak a peek at the Mangox. "I mean, my master, has been looking forward to the trip."

The capo stepped back for a moment to address her. "Do not worry, lovely one. You and your master will be on your way soon enough."

"We will meet you on your outpost," I said with finality. The more the bastard stared at Jane, the hotter my ire grew.

"Wonderful!" The capo clapped his paws, gave us a quick half bow, and headed back to the airlock. "We shall see you there."

As the airlock closed and their ship disconnected from ours, the little captain walked out from behind me. She rubbed the back of her neck as she looked up at me. "Ah, so, that went well."

I grabbed her by the hips and pulled her to me. The lace of her outfit tickled my palms. I wanted nothing more than to tear it off her. "Just remember what I said before, ljona." I kissed her hard, my tongue diving in to explore her depths. When her breaths turned to pants, I paused only to remind her of what my hearts wanted to be true. "You are mine."

6

Jane

I AM THE CAPTAIN OF THE MOONBASE. I TUGGED AT THE cups of my halter top, attempting to position the skimpy fabric around the exposed sides of my breasts. *This is not how I should be meeting a new intelligent species.* Although the jury was out on whether the Mangox qualified, since they were clearly engaging in behavior that should be outlawed by any species with an iota of sense.

"Don't fidget, ljona." Tor draped his arm over my shoulders, a sense of warmth and comfort infusing me with the action. I found myself liking the sensations and being close to the big warrior. Under normal circumstances, that realization would have sent me running. But as it was, I relished the feelings.

"I'm not fidgeting." I straightened and wrapped my arm around his waist to make it easier to walk side-by-side. "I'm situating."

As the ramp lowered, we prepared to enter the lion's den. The outpost had been less than fifteen minutes away with the help of the ship's hyperdrive. Unfortunately, the Mangox had similar technology, so we matched paced with them as we followed their massive vessel to the coordinates. I wasn't sure what I expected from an alien station, but what I got was… not it.

The landing platform opened to an enormous energy dome. The barrier allowed ships in and out while keeping a suitable atmosphere for visitors to walk unimpeded. That wasn't as surprising as the variety of said visitors. I clutched Tor's waist a bit harder. "Who are all these people?"

"Traders." The commander tightened his grip on my shoulders. "That's the nice way to put it."

"What's the not nice way?" I asked, trying to keep my jaw shut. The breath of different species blew my mind.

"Scoundrels, ruffians, miscreants," he shrugged those muscled shoulders, ripe with tension, "take your pick."

"Lovely." I sighed. My senses perked up as I observed a yellow blob of an alien with one large singular eye in its…head? It was hard to tell as its entire body appeared the consistency of jelly, and it was shaped like a…well a…I guess banana would be the most apt description. "What is that?"

Tor caught the direction of my gaze. "Cellions. They're psychedelic dealers."

"I'm sorry, the banana jelly is a drug dealer?" My eyes widened like twin teacup saucers.

"The manner of that translation is interesting, little captain." He snorted. "But, yes, essentially they are."

I took a good look around the landing bay as we headed toward the interior of the outpost. A gray-skinned creature with four long horns and hoofed feet walked beside an insect-like alien with four arms and creepy antennas. They spoke of a slave rebellion, and the downfall of the trade on that planet. I smiled inwardly, rooting for anyone who rose up against oppressors.

"Be careful where you place your sights," Tor whispered to me. "Remember you're posing as a slave. Do not be too bold with your gaze."

A lick of rage ran through me, but I clamped it down with effort. It wasn't the commander's fault we were in this situation. I might not like it, but I had to act the part for both our sakes. "I understand."

He hugged me to his side. His mouth at my ear. "You're doing well, Ijona. We'll be as quick as we can and free of this soon."

His praise helped ease some of my nervous energy. It also caused heat to pool low. I clamped my thighs together, making it a tad awkward to walk.

"There you are, my new friends." Capo Mulo emerged from a doorway on the opposite side of the landing bay, waving us over with his beefy arm. The Mangox were an intimidating bunch, I'd give them that. The capo's bodyguards had to be at least eight feet tall, and the leader stood at Tor's height. Their arms were as thick as their legs with ample muscle in all their limbs. The long, thin snout at the center of their faces covered their gaping mouths, but I caught a glimpse of the rows of sharp teeth inside. The capo greeted us with one of those toothy smiles. "Come! Now, we drink."

Tor's hold tightened impossibly more, almost to the point of pain. I squeezed his side, and he loosened his grip a fraction. Yet, his body radiated tension, like a coiled snake poised to strike. His voice, on the other hand, revealed none of the strain, as he said, "Lead on, Capo."

"That a male." Mulo nodded and motioned to one of his underlings. "Go and tell our friends we'll be entertaining in the rhapsodic chamber."

My mind whirled with possibilities of what could take place in such a named area. I wasn't sure I wanted to find out, but it seemed I had little choice.

The capo led us through a dark, spiraling hallway that gradually inclined. The walls were rounded and smooth as if constructed of a solid piece of black granite. Circular pods, about as large as my hand, alighted the path every few feet. We passed a series of doors with glowing symbols on the outside, but my babbler translation unit could not decipher the patterns. When we rose what had to be several stories from the landing bay, the Mangox leader stopped before an enormous pane of frosted glass. It was as wide as Tor was tall and at least double his height. As if lit from within, it shifted in color from one moment to the next, showcasing purples, blues, reds, and deep oranges.

"Ah, here we are." The capo placed his palm against the pane. The glass brightened to a brilliant magenta hue, then it slid into two pieces. Each part glided into the wall, disappearing behind the dark stone. "The other guests will be waiting."

With the glass gone, the room beyond it took shape. Structured as a large oval with curved walls, it mirrored the hall. It reminded me of a chicken's egg, only if it had been squashed and stretched like putty. A long, rectangular stone table ran down the center of the room. On it rested goblets and plates with what I imagined was food, although I recognized none of it. Spread out from the table were a wide variety of seating areas, from simple pillows to swinging chairs and woven baskets suspended from the ceiling. The aliens inside them came in every form conceivable as well.

"Here now." Mulo motioned to us. "Choose whatever is appropriate for you."

I had to admit having the different seating arrangements certainly made it convenient for his guests. From the purple and green slime creature hanging in a bowl-like seat to the tall and thin giraffe-like alien who sat on a flat cushion in the corner, the capo knew how to accommodate the unique physiques of the differing species.

"How about there, Jane?" Tor whispered to me and pointed to a chair with its back to the wall. It had two distinct cushions and appeared to glide in a circle. It reminded me a bit of a porch swing that my grandmother talked about from the old days.

I nodded and kept my voice low. "Yes, it's close enough to the exit without allowing anyone behind us."

"My thoughts too." Taking my arm once more, we headed for the seat.

The two-person chair did in fact swing, and it took a bit of doing to get comfortable in it. But after Tor pulled me closer so that my back rested against his chest, it worked well.

"Partake, my friends," Mulo addressed the crowd, which at my count numbered about thirty or so. "Eat, drink, and may the festivities begin!"

A rumble of music poured from unseen holo-speakers. It flowed about the room in rhythmic beats accompanied by a flute instrument. Cube-shaped robots gathered food and drink from the table, portioning it and floating on air to deliver it to the attendees. One such droid gave us a platter with brown mash, blue meat, purple vegetables, and sparkling bread along with two goblets of a pungent smelling drink.

I held my nose and asked the robotic waiter, "May I have some water?"

The droid blinked twice without answering, then dashed to the far side of the room and through a doorway, which I assumed led to the kitchens.

"Was that a no?" I glanced over my shoulder at Tor.

He shrugged and pulled a canteen from his vest. "Here, drink this." He handed it to me and placed the goblets on the floor beside our swinging chair. "Only this."

I tipped it back, allowing enough liquid to wet my dry throat. "Good call. Who knows what's in those drinks. Do we dare try the food?"

"I recognize some of it, although it wouldn't be my first choice." He ripped off a chunk of the blue meat and purple root-like vegetable. "These two are safe. The other stuff I'm unsure of."

"Let's stick to what you know." I picked a piece of each and held it before my mouth. "Well, here goes." The meat tasted like burnt chicken and the veggie was like an…apple? Pear? It was somewhere between the two. Confusing, but not bad. "It's not the worst I've ever had."

Tor ate his portion and took a swig from the canteen. "That about sums up the flavor. Neither good, nor bad."

I wanted to ask the commander where the food came from. I was particularly curious about the blue meat, but a harsh gong broke our dinner conversation. Mulo had climbed atop the table at its center. The gong was a star-shaped hunk of glowing metal that descended from the ceiling and hung above his head. He used an enormous club to bash it. "And for our event this evening we have," the capo dropped the club and raised an ornate goblet to the audience, "lustrara tempara."

Excited murmurs and chatter erupted amongst the attendees. I spun in our seat so I could look at Tor. "Do I want to know?" I raised a brow at him.

The grimace on his face was answer enough.

Mulo's voice rose above the crowd, "Yes! It will be a grand affair." He chugged the contents of the goblet, then threw the empty cup to the floor. It clanged as it landed and rolled onto a nearby pillow. "Before we get to the main course, I have an appetizer to wet your desires." He held his beefy arm before him and swung it toward the back of the room. "Behold."

A spotlight glowed a bright, golden hue toward the far end of the table, highlighting a trio of aliens. Two of the group had aquatic features with large fins on the sides of their heads, bulbous eyes, webbed fingers, and fishtails. Their skin was a slick silvery-blue, and with the exception of slight differences in their facial features, they could have passed for twins. The third was smaller than the other two with long black hair, purple-hued skin, smaller eyes, and a set of tentacles instead of legs —or a fish tail.

"A peorna pod." Tor sucked in a breath as he leaned closer to the edge of our seat. "I've heard rumors of their kind. But they're highly isolated on their home world." His arms went around me as if without conscious thought. "What are they doing here?"

"I'd imagine it has something to do with this loose-trah event, no?" I held onto his forearms to balance in the chair.

He frowned. "Lustrara tempara."

"Yeah, that." I squeezed his arms. "And what is that?"

A grumble vibrated in his chest, the sensation tickling my back. "It's a—"

The music rose again, louder than before. The drumbeats punctuated the flute notes like a pulse beneath the melody. The golden light brightened, and the trio began to dance. The purple alien, who I believed was female, waved her tentacles in a sensuous display, as if each undulated to their own rhythm. The silver-blue pair, who I guessed were male, pressed her tentacles to their humanoid chests and stroked them with long, webbed fingers.

"Marvelous, aren't they?" The capo shouted over the music. He had taken a seat at the opposite end of the table, not far from ours. It was a mammoth, lush cushion that hung on invisible wires and molded to his body as he half-reclined. "A true splendor! And a testament to my gang."

"They work for the Mangox?" I cupped my hand around my mouth and scooted up to ask the question in Tor's ear.

He held me as I balanced in his lap, and said back, "I doubt it's a congenial arrangement."

"No, Rhonar." The capo snapped in our direction. "Patience," he waved a paw at us, "that's for later."

I pulled a face, my nose scrunching. "What's he talking about?"

Tor glanced at where I knelt in his lap. The position did appear suggestive, but what did that Mangox bastard think we were going to do? A sinking sensation plopped in my gut. I moved to sit beside the commander and turned my attention back to the trio. The knot in my stomach tightened as the peorna pod's display had grown…graphic.

"Is *that* what he thought?" I shouted to Tor. He didn't answer, and I didn't look at him. My gaze was glued on the aliens.

The pair had each taken a place before the female, one behind her and one in front. The front male was kneeling between her tentacles, right at the spot where a human female's pussy would be. His ear fins flapped vigorously as his face was buried below. The male behind her had flipped his tail underneath her and rocked her on it. His amphibious lips sucked on the side of her neck, leaving marks in the wake of his touch.

Their actions grew more frantic as the music rose to a crescendo. The males emitted a high-pitched frequency that aligned with the drumbeats. The female shrieked a note that matched the flute-sounds. Then, without warning, all three stiffened, holding their respective notes, until the last beat. When it ended, they collapsed onto each other, a mess of tails and tentacles splayed on the table.

"Wonderful! Wonderful!" Mulo rose from his seat, clapping his paws. Much of the audience did as well, stomping or howling their praise.

I glanced at Tor, who wore a stoic expression.

"And now, for the main course." A group of aliens emerged from beyond the back wall. It was only then I realized a black curtain hung there, separating the spaces. Three bear-like creatures with wide hips and dead eyes walked toward the capo. A lecherous smile spread across his face. "Come, my lovelies." Grabbing the closest to him, he pushed her onto the swinging cushion. Then, he placed the other two on either side of it. "Let the festivities commence!"

As if unbound from invisible chains, the crowd began to move. Several pairs rearranged their seating, while other groups of threes and fours claimed part of the table, the floor, or swinging platforms. Moans and groans quickly took the place of the music, which quieted to a low throbbing beat. Clothes were strewn about the floor.

I had no idea where to look. "I'm, ah…"

"Be at ease, ljona." Tor grabbed my hand and squeezed. "Nothing will happen to you. Understand?" His gray-purple eyes burned into mine. "No one will come near you."

A bellowing roar echoed from the capo who was ramming the smaller Mangox female from behind. The other two stroked his furry balls and thrust a dull claw between his ass cheeks. He finished by pushing the first onto her stomach and ignoring the other two. When his beady-eyes turned to me, I shuddered.

"Ah, Commander," his limp cock, which had been hidden in a pouch of skin before, dangled freely as he stalked toward us, "why do you not partake in the lustrara tempara? It is an insult to the gods to stand idle when such temptations abound."

"Our mating rituals are not for prying eyes, Capo." Tor rose at the Mangox leader's approach and blocked me from view. I peeked between his legs to gets a glimpse of the interaction.

"Of course!" Mulo's smile did not reach his eyes. "But the lovely one is not your mate, now is she? Surely, you can participate with a mere slave."

The commander's body vibrated with unspent anger. I laid a hand on his back, hoping to help him maintain calm.

The capo continued, "Perhaps, if she's being unreasonable, you might be willing to sell her." A barking laugh emanated from the Mangox that chilled my blood. "I am quite talented at breaking recalcitrant slaves."

The deep, snarling growl that passed Tor's lips was not that of a sentient being, but a beast on the edge of ripping apart his prey. His feet flew faster than I could track as he grabbed the capo by the shirt and held him a foot off the floor. He bared fangs at the bastard, and said one word, "Never."

7

Tor

RAGE CONSUMED ME, FIERCER THAN THE VOID, FASTER than the emotional whirlwinds. Like a wildfire it burned me from the inside out. I wanted nothing more than to tear apart the bastard's throat with my teeth. His disgusting pebbled eyes bulged from his head. He clawed at my forearms, leaving red slices in my skin.

I felt nothing. Nothing but the fires within.

"Put him down. Please, put him down." Heat surrounded my waist. *Jane.* Her golden arms were wrapped around me. "You can't do this. We'll never get out of here if you do."

I glanced around the room at her words. The lustrara tempara continued, but the capo's guards were cutting a path through the crowd. I could take them down, but would we make it off the outpost? *Crex.* With more strength of will than I'd imagined possible, I placed the capo on his feet.

He stuttered and coughed before coming to himself. "For the stars, Rhonar, you are a surly flok." Straightening, he grabbed his com unit from his belt— which he hadn't bother to do away with during his earlier dalliance—and spoke into it. "Stand down. A minor tiff during negotiations."

The guards stopped in their tracks, eyed the capo, and then returned to their prior posts. I crossed my arms over my chest, not wanting to give a hint of my surprise. No matter my actions, this Mangox didn't seem phased. *Why?* I hadn't consciously used my power while holding the bastard by the neck, but the sensations flowed through me, nonetheless. The male had few strengths, beyond ambition that took the form of ample greed, and several weaknesses, such as coveting others. I suspected the truth, but now with my abilities, his intentions crystallized in my mind. *Jane. He wants to claim Jane.* I struggled not to let my ire show. I'd not allow him to succeed.

"Truly I've never seen a male so attached to his slave." Mulo waved back toward his harem. "Not that it doesn't happen. I was quite fond of Parla there." He glanced at the Mangox female on his seat. Hatred shone in her eyes, but the capo didn't appear to notice—or care. "She was loyal for so long, until she started an affair with one of my guards." He sighed. "The poor male had to be put down, of course. And now she must be punished regularly. It's such a shame."

I bit my tongue at the disgusting display. Jane gasped behind me.

Misunderstanding her reaction, he said to her, "Oh I know, my dear! Awful, isn't it?" He shifted to the side, trying to capture a view of her. "You would never behave so reprehensible, would you?"

"My ljona is loyal to me." I sidestepped to block her from his sight.

"Yes, Master." The little captain rose from the swinging chair but kept behind me. "I am yours alone."

Drav it. I could not be affected by her words. It was an act to save us in this situation. But crex it all, if it didn't heat my blood, replacing the fires of rage with pure desire. "You see, Capo? She is mine."

The twisted grin pulled his snout toward the ceiling. "Yes, yes. I can see that." He snapped his fingers, and the music which had quieted during the "main event," as he called it, rose to a steady beat. The attendees' moans grew louder too. "But since you deny me a sale, I must insist on your participation." His beady-eyes narrowed to slits. "No one comes to my party and stands idle."

"Yes, Capo." Jane stepped to the side, revealing part of her body to the Mangox. I growled. "Master, I *want* to join in."

My jaw dropped. I whirled around to face her. In the time I'd known her, I'd learned that while she was a fierce fighter. Yet, when it came to more intimate matters, I did not imagine such boldness. While I'd happily take her anywhere, in any way she desired, I doubted she'd want the same. And it was not that simple. She was my mate, my Truxoria. Although, I'd denied claiming her, if we joined together, if we crexed, the bond would solidify.

I haven't told her the truth. I struggled to keep my growl at bay. *And I don't want these crexers seeing her.* "No, little…" I'd almost called her captain, which would not do for a slave. "Little female. You are not for their amusement."

"Rhonar," the capo used my species name in a deadly threat, "do not test me."

"Please, Master," she pitched her voice higher and clapped her hands, "it looks like so much fun."

Lies. The brightness in her eyes told the truth far more than her words. But my little captain was putting on a brave front, pushing herself out of her comfort zone to save our skins. I had to come up with a plan to honor that courage. "Hmm, my ljona," I brushed my knuckles across her cheek, "you want me then?"

The scent of her arousal filled my nose, an aroma more enticing than any in the universe. While she might not like the situation, she could not fake her desire. "Yes, please. I want to participate in the capo's party."

"Hah!" Mulo barked behind us. "You see, then? Your slave wants to enjoy herself." He slapped me on the back. "Make it a good show for the gods." His words were like poison to my ears. "We'll be keeping an eye on you." He tapped his com and did a slow take of the room, letting his gaze linger on each of his guards. Then, he headed back toward his harem, pushing the next female in line on his seat.

"Crexer," I cursed as my hands balled into fists.

A ragged breath sputtered from Jane. "It's okay, Tor." She put her hands on my chest and rose on her tiptoes. "I can…" She shook her head. "No, *we* can do this."

"My little captain." I held her by the waist, wanting both to pick her up and push her away. The emotions warred within me. "You don't know what you're asking."

She guffawed at that. Her arm swept around the room. "I think I have a pretty good idea."

"No." I picked her up so that she had to wrap her legs around me. "You don't."

Her fingers dove into my hair. She yanked my head back to meet my eyes. "Then, show me."

JANE

This was the definition of madness. It had to be. I was in the commander's arms, pretending to be his slave, trapped in a room with a bunch of horny aliens, and begging him to…

Well, okay, I wasn't exactly sure what I was asking for, but I wanted *something*. Anything. I'd never been so turned on in my life. I didn't consider myself a voyeur, and truthfully, I didn't think it was the aliens, although the sounds of the kinky group stuff were kind of hot.

But no. It was this alien warrior. His fucking growls, and his protective ways, melted me into a pile of mush. And heated me up.

"I want you, Tor," I whispered in his ear and bit the enticing lobe. "I need it."

"Jane," he said my name like a curse and a prayer mixed together. "It's not that simple. I can't mate with you."

"It's fine, if we both want it." I tightened my grip in my hair. "I mean, it's not ideal. But as long as its mutual…" I let my unspoken question linger. If the commander didn't want me, then I was making a damn fool of myself.

"I want you, ljona. Believe me." He shifted his grip to my ass and pulled me against him. "Can you feel how much?"

"Yes." Oh, fuck yes, I could. His cock was hard as steel beneath his pants. He didn't have on his usual leathers. These were the loose sparring pants of earlier, and they were as thin as my lingerie. It was amazing.

"Feel how hard for you, I am, my Truxoria?" He thrust against me, his thick cockhead bumping my clit. "I'd crex you for days, if I could."

"Then," I gasped for breath, my body drawing tight as a bow, "why don't you?" I didn't care who in the universe was watching. I wanted him more than fucking air. It wasn't rational. None of this was. But as much as my mind told me I barely knew this alien, my body said I wanted to know more.

"I'll explain everything to you, but not here. Not like this." He placed me in our swinging chair and climbed in beside me—but in the opposite direction. "Now, put your legs over my head, little captain. Straddle my face. I want to taste that sweet pussy like I've been dying to."

"Oh fuck!" I moaned at his hot words. Doing as he commanded, I put my knees on either side of his shoulders. I had to face away from him, which meant all I had to do was bend over to reach that glorious cock. I smiled at that. Resting my hands on his legs, I leaned over him. But as I was preparing my attack, he struck first.

His muscular arms wrapped around my thighs and pulled me wider. The action meant my pussy came closer to his seeking tongue. Pushing my panties to one side with his thumb, he ran it over my outer lips and blew cool air on my overheated sex. Then, he began a slow torture, licking my thighs, my lips, and the crease of each leg. He carefully avoided my clit. I squirmed in his grasp, my body on fire. He slapped my ass cheek. "No, ljona. Hold still."

Not to be outdone, I bent lower so my face rested on his thigh. I crept my fingers under the hem of his pants. He groaned. "What are you doing?"

"You're not the only one who wants this." I slipped his waistband over his hips, and… "Whoa!" He had two cocks. Well, not quite. But he had a smaller mushroom-shaped appendage at the base of his shaft that curved above it. It reminded me of a popular sex toy. The main cock was beyond intimidating. I gasped, wondering idly how I'd get any of it into my mouth, let alone my pussy.

"I can feel your tension, my Truxoria." He ceased his teasing of my wet pussy lips and stroked my back. "What is wrong?"

I stared at him through my legs. "Wrong? Nothing. You're just huge!"

He chuckled at that, continuing to pet me as if calming a startled animal. "You do not have to worry. When I take you, you'll be well prepared." As if to put proof to his words, he sucked my clit at last and thrust one long, thick finger into my core.

I screamed. "Tor!"

He paused, taking his mouth from me, and slapped my ass again. With his finger still inside me, my pussy clenched hard. "Remember, it's Master."

"Yes, Master." I'd call him whatever he wanted. My clit throbbed like a second heartbeat. He slid his tongue around it, creating slow circles that drove me wild. I had to attempt something to get back to an even playing field.

Leaning over him again, I palmed his shaft with both hands and licked along that top cock. I couldn't get my fingers all the way around him, but it didn't matter. His hips bucked, and I smiled. My advantage didn't last, however, as he redoubled his efforts on my clit and pushed a second finger inside me. Thrusting them in and out slowly, he built a glorious tempo. I matched his rhythm, pumping his cock.

"Jane," he said, removing his fingers, before he plunged his tongue deep inside. Then, it vibrated. His tongue fucking vibrated.

I screamed. My pussy was dripping, but he swallowed every bit, as if he couldn't get enough. I tried to keep pace, sucking his top cock and stroking the other, but he was pushing me over the edge. Without warning, he removed his tongue and thrust his fingers back inside. Using that vibrating beauty, he clamped his lips over my clit and sucked. The vibrations of his tongue against my clit, his lips wrapped around it, and his fingers deep in my pussy were too much.

"Master! Master!" I cried as my back arched. My legs shook from the force of my orgasm. I squeezed my eyes shut as tears formed in the corners. The sensations swirled around and through me, the waves of pleasure overloading my system. I'd never experienced anything like it. I wanted to crawl out of my skin while equally never wanting it to end. "Tor."

"I've got you, my ljona." He held me through it, stroking my thighs. "You're all right."

I slumped against him. My hair brushed his skin. But when my cheek nuzzled his cocks, I perked up. I might have felt spent to the bone, but I wanted to drive him wild as much as he did to me. With a sense of renewed purpose, I brought my lips to his cock head and sucked.

"Jane," he groaned my name and tried to pull away. But I had him. I used one hand to tease his top cock while my mouth worked the full one. I couldn't take much of him, but I used my other hand to wrap around as much as I could at the base. His cock head bobbed in my mouth. I licked it lovingly and sucked it like a candy. When I switched to cup his balls, he nearly bucked off the seat.

I let loose his cock to look at him over my shoulder. "It's your turn, commander. Come in my mouth." I licked a line down the center of his shaft. "I want it." Then, I returned my lips to his cock head and hollowed my cheeks. The motions pushed him over the edge. His body tensed and his cum hit the back of my throat. My eyes widened at the flavor. I hadn't been with a ton of men—Earth was lacking in them after all—but I'd never imagined the taste could be…well…good. *Like cinnamon and coffee.*

Licking my lips, I set him free. He was still hard. I climbed over his chest to spin around, so we were face-to-face. "Are you okay?"

"Little captain," he laughed, a deep bellow, "I'm more than okay."

"Then, why are you," I pointed toward his erect cock, "you know, hard?"

"Why would I not be, ljona?" He lifted one of my legs to draw it over his hip. "Do Terran males soften after one encounter?"

I failed at keeping the shock off my face. I couldn't see my reflection, but I knew it. My cheeks were hot, and the tips of my ears practically burned. "Ah…yeah."

"That's a pity," he said with what sounded like true sincerity. "Once is never enough when it comes to pleasure with one's mate."

"Right," I said, not knowing quite how to answer. So, I changed the subject. "And what about your second cock? Human men definitely do *not* have that."

"Ah, you mean my crux." He motioned to it. "It is for you, my Truxoria. To stimulate you during mating."

My eyes bugged out of my head. *Hell on a stick.* There was one hundred percent no way that I could hide my surprise on that revelation. "Got it." I tucked my head to his chest, not wanting to think too much. I'd always been one for cuddling after the more vigorous stuff.

Unfortunately, our reprieve came to an end when Mulo's voice shouted from across the room. "Now that was most entertaining, Rhonar." The bastard clapped his meaty paws. "A well showing for our party."

Tor vibrated beside me, and not in the good way. He stuffed his cock—and crux—into his pants and readjusted the waistband. Then, he sat up, careful not to spill me over the side of our swinging chair. I rose with him. Like him, I was itching to give this capo a what-for, but we had to get off this outpost in one piece and get on with our mission. So, I bit my tongue, and called out to the Mangox.

"Thank you, Capo." I stood up and bowed like I imagined a good, little slave would do. But in my mind I was picturing a series of deaths for the bastard, each more painful than the last. I kept my voice higher pitched as I said, "Master and I are so pleased we could join your…" I hesitated, struggling to find a suitable word that wasn't orgy.

"Your lustrara tempara," Tor filled in for me. He rose next to me, lending me his strength with his presence. "It is a spectacle unlike any I've seen before."

The capo shot us a toothy smile. Anyone that didn't know the Rhonar commander might have thought his words were a compliment, but I knew better. I may not have known him long, but my bullshit meter was finely tuned to him. I hid my laugh behind a cough.

Mulo didn't seem to notice anything amiss. "Indeed," he flapped his meaty paw, "indeed, it is." The capo eyed me in a manner that had the hairs on my neck rising. "Now, let us retire to our seats. Dessert will arrive soon." A ball of dread tightened my gut. Foreboding filled me.

The capo snapped his fingers and the music shifted. A languorous tune, more suited to one of Dr. Harper's yoga sessions in our holo-studio, filled the room. The soft chiming notes reminded me of Grace's soothing voice as she'd guide the moonbase crew through a gentle flow. *"Now, let it all go, and breathe into the movement."* The memory choked my throat. And the warning in my heart beat strong.

Something was going to happen.

Reaching for Tor's hand, I thread my fingers through his. I didn't look at him as I spoke, too afraid he'd see the emotions written on my face. "Promise me. No matter what happens, you will complete this mission."

8

Tor

Jane's voice rang with a deadly calm, but her words set my hearts racing. "*We* will complete this mission, ljona." I tucked my hand under her chin and turned her face to mine. "That I vow to you."

She shot me a weak smile as she reclaimed our seat.

I knelt beside the chair on one knee and took her hand. Her breath hitched. "From henceforth, I am yours." I placed my free hand against my sternum. "My kedara, my life's blood, flows for you. My body is your shield. I swear no harm will come to you, lest I am fallen." I kissed her knuckles. "You are safe in my care."

"Tor," she whispered my name like a benediction. Her ocean blue eyes glistened. "I don't know what to say." I rose as she spoke. "No one has ever made me a promise like that."

Sliding in next to her, I grasped her waist and placed her in my lap where she belonged. "I am glad I'm the first, then." My throat tightened, emotions squeezing my chest. *And I will be your last.*

Tapping the tip of my nose with her pointer finger, she laughed. "Still the cocky commander."

I drew her waggling finger into my mouth, gently running my tongue around it. With her soft intake of breath and blossoming arousal, I would have happily taken her for round two. But sadly, we had a job to do. I set her free and spoke in her ear. "We need a distraction to escape the party unnoticed."

"I agree." Her wild hair tickled my neck as she replied. "And it has to be before this dessert happens. I have a bad feeling about it."

"All right, let's decide on a strategy to—"

The gong reverberated through the room, rung this time by one of the waiter bots from earlier. Mulo remained on his platform with his harem. One of his guards strutted to the center of the table with a piece of fabric in hand. "And now, the great Capo," he motioned toward the Mangox leader, who simply nodded at him in answer, "presents the final course of the lustrara tempara." An array of bots and aliens emerged from behind the back curtain. Each held a similar piece of fabric between their claws, hands, or robotic arms. The guard raised his sash over his head, and those assembled behind him mirrored the movement. "Behold your dessert!"

The crowd went into an uproar, hooting, howling, and shouting their praise. Cries of "Capo! Capo!" went up as the fabric was distributed to the guests.

"Tor, I don't like this." Jane's hands dug into my side.

I didn't have the same fear as her, but anger slid through me at her distress. I wanted to murder whoever caused it. "Here you are." A bot handed me a piece of purple fabric, and then a second orange one. "And for your lady."

"Thanks," I mumbled, unsure what was happening. I'd heard of lustrara tempara before. The hedonistic parties were legendary in the Meta Sector and rumors abounded, but I'd never been to one. I preferred my encounters on the more intimate side, and now that I had a mate, well, all I needed was her.

"Now, my friends," the capo rose with his strip of purple tied around his head, "to those with slaves in attendance, you'll want to tie the orange sash around their eyes." He motioned to one of the females in his harem, who was blindfolded with the orange strip. "Any wearing purple are in command. Those who wear orange," he cocked his head toward us, staring pointedly at Jane, "are up for the taking. Claim your treats!"

I surged to my feet. Nothing would stop me from unleashing my rage on this bastard. "You dare." I flung both sashes to the floor. Another gong rang free as if punctuating my ire.

Jane rose and balled her hands into fists, prepping for the oncoming fight.

The Mangox crexer had the gall to cast us a grin while he reached for his com unit. I walked toward him, assessing my prey. Jane was in step beside me. As we got closer, a crisp communique came through his unit, "Boss, we have a situation."

His malignant gaze remained on us as he spoke into the com, "*I* am about to have a situation here. You need to bring all the guards."

"But Capo, we've received a call from the pleasure cruiser." The static ticked up a notch, but the messenger's voice remained clear. "They've had some type of an emergency, and the ship is in self-destruct mode."

"*WHAT?*" Mulo's roar threw metaphorical ice water on the participants. The music stopped abruptly, and all attention turned to the capo. "Incompetent floks." The Mangox leader whirled away from us, too lost in his call to care about our approach.

I didn't give a damn. I wanted to knock his crexing head off. I'd been in too many battles to count, but I'd never felt this rush of emotion, this bloodthirsty drive. I'd fought on adrenaline and duty. Now, I wanted to burn down the world in my mate's name.

"Tor." *My* name on her lips had my head spinning—the mix of primal needs a heady concoction. "We have to use this chance."

The capo paced the room in agitation. "You tell them that ship cost a fortune, and they have no business doing anything without my consent."

"He's distracted. He won't notice our absence." My ljona tugged my arm toward the exit.

She was right. Of course, she was right. I'd have recommended the most logical choice in any mission scenario, but it didn't satisfy the craving inside me. "I want to kill him."

Her long, slender fingers reached for my face and stroked the scruff on my chin. "I know, Commander, so do I." A shout from the capo drew both our gazes. "He deserves it for his lechery and for holding those poor women captive. But we have a duty to uphold to our people." The Mangox leader grumbled and stomped across the room. "We need to leave. Now."

I hated it. In any other situation, I would have taken on the challenge. But I couldn't. I could not defend my Truxoria's honor, and that ate at me more than anything. "He dared to dishonor you, Jane."

She snorted. "If you had any idea how much human women have put up with from our men over the millennia, you would not be worried about that asshole." Thumbing a finger toward Mulo, she laughed. Then, her gaze shifted to his harem, and then my…vest? "Besides, he'll get what's coming to him." She poked beneath my vest. "May I have one of your knives?"

I'd deny her nothing. "They're daggers, but yes." I pulled one free I thought would fit her hand best and held the hilt out to her.

"Thank you." A wicked smile tugged her lips at the corners. "I know just what to do with it."

Heading for the capo's platform, I followed as Jane walked up to the Mangox harem. "Hello there." She inclined her head in greeting, while I kept watch around us. The Mangox females removed the sashes from their eyes. "I have a gift for you, Parla." She raised her chin to stare into the eyes of the slave female Mulo had spoken of by name—the one who had an affair with one of his guards. "If you'd like, you can keep this, and perhaps," holding my dagger between her and Parla, she angled her body, so the weapon was hidden from view by any onlookers, "put it to good use."

Parla's coal eyes widened, her long, thin snout rising toward her forehead. "Your Master allows such a present?"

"I'll confess to you, friend." Jane leaned conspiratorially to whisper in the Mangox's ear. "He's not my master. He's my," she glanced over her shoulder at me, "my partner."

I was far more than that, but it was not the time to reveal such things.

"You are lucky, then." Claiming the dagger in her paw, she used the orange sash to conceal it around her waist. The neutral expression on her face revealed little, but a deep hatred burned in her eyes as she glared across the room at the capo. When her gaze returned to Jane, it softened. "I thank you for this gift. It is well received." Motioning behind the platform, she added, "If you place your hand on the wall over there, you'll find it opens to a stairwell that runs to the base of the outpost." The capo's tantrum grew louder, and people began to shuffle toward the glass door exit. "You should leave that way."

"Thank you!" Jane grasped Parla's paw and shook it twice.

The Mangox female startled at first, but then a small genuine smile, the first I'd seen from her, stretched over her mouth. "You are welcome…"

"Jane." My ljona supplied. "I hope we meet again."

"The universe is a mysterious place." Parla sat on the edge of the platform, the two other females flanking her. "It may be so. Now go, my new friend Jane, and may the stars be with you."

The trio of females helped hide our retreat as we circled around them toward the back as Parla had instructed. I put my hand to the wall. Light traced around my fingers and palm, and then split off to create a rectangular shape. Within beats, a doorway appeared.

"Whoa." Jane inched forward to peer inside. "That was cool. And Parla was right. It's a stairwell. Let's go."

"Wait." I held her back with a hand on her shoulder. I grabbed another two daggers from my vest, placing one in her palm. "Let me go first."

She scoffed and rolled her eyes. "Fine, cocky commander, lead on."

I bent down to ensure she saw the desire in my eyes, the same heat that flicked across my skin. "I'm starting to like when you call me that, Jane."

"Yeah, well." A hint of her arousal perfumed the air. I licked my lips. She waved me onward. "Just go, okay?"

I laughed, but soon my mirth receded. The stairs through this hidden chamber did not have the same illumination as the main one. I could see well enough in the dark to determine the edge of the stairs and the rounded center column, but I knew Terrans lacked such ability. "Give me your hand."

"Thanks," she gasped. Her stride was measured behind me. "It's so creepy in here. Our footsteps echo too loudly, and I can't see a thing."

"We'll be fine, my Truxoria. Just hold on to me." Every step brought us closer to leaving this draving place and getting on with our mission.

Silence reigned for a click between us, before she said, "Why do you call me that?" She sucked in a breath, the air hissing through her teeth. "It's a new word, not your ljona creature, or your silly little captain nickname." Her hands dug into my sides as we walked. "It's more reverent too, when you say it."

I tensed under her touch. *Crex it.* I had to tell her the truth, admit she was my mate. But how in the void did I cross that space between us? *Do I deserve to?* Doubt lingered in me. We hadn't completed the mission. I desired Jane, but I had my duty. Would it be wrong to claim her now? If we failed. *That's not an option.*

"Tor," her fingers stroked my back as if soothing a skittering beast. "It's all right. You don't have to say anything." She stepped around me as we came to the final landing. Light filtered in from beyond the doorway. She stood on tiptoe and cupped my cheek. "Tell me when you're ready."

"I will, Jane." I claimed her hand and kissed the back. "I promise you."

"Good." She chuckled, tugging her fingers free of my hold. "Now, let's get out of here. And finish our mission, huh?'

"Yes," I agreed wholeheartedly and handed her a sheath. "Hide your dagger for now. We don't want to bring unnecessary attention to ourselves."

"Right," she said, attaching the sheath to her thigh garter and placing the dagger inside. Jane was beyond mere words of beauty to me. Her courage, dedication to her people, and strength as a leader, all drew me to her. Yet, I had to admit, my dagger strapped to her leg was hot as crex. She smirked as if knowing my thoughts.

I took a beat to collect my wayward mind and plan our exit across the outpost. Stalking through the doorway, I noted the same mix of aliens from earlier. Every thief, swindler, and pirate in the sector congregated in this place. I had to get us to our ship and through the energy dome barrier with as much stealth as possible. The Mangox were currently occupied, but they were not the only bastards we had to worry about on this accursed station.

Jane kept her head down and her gaze on the floor as we zigzagged over the outpost floor. But I could tell she was alert. Tension radiated from her as we progressed. Our space fighter rested on the far side of the landing bay, away from the trading ships.

"Not much further." I pitched my voice low to avoid any overhearing ears. Most of the station visitors were busy bartering for whatever contraband they'd brought to trade. But Jane would be a prize to any slaver. We had to stay vigilant.

"Rhonar are the scum of the galaxy!" A shout sounded too nearby for comfort. I turned toward the noise, Jane following my lead. A gray-skinned alien emerged from the crowd. "You should all be put down."

As the stranger came closer, I noted his species. "Craxion."

"I saw him before with a bug-alien," Jane whispered, her hair forming a curtain to hide her face. "He was talking about a slave rebellion."

"Yes," I replied for her ears alone. "That's the planet where we first encountered Terrans, where your scientist Ava was saved."

"Fuck." Jane put a hand on her dagger.

"Not yet." I crossed my arms over my chest, palming my own daggers concealed beneath my vest. "Let's see if he's ready for a fight or all bluster."

"All bark, no bite." She nodded, her foot gliding seamlessly into her fighting stance. "He seems the type."

When the Craxion stood within striking distance of us, I cataloged his appearance. He wore no shoes but needed none with his powerful hooves. Four curved horns sprouted from his hairless head. He was covered in an animal hide from neck to thigh as was the style of his people. Wicked claws sprouted from his hands. None of that concerned me save for the blaster attached to his belt.

"You, Rhonar," he spat my species name like a curse, "have decimated the economy of Craxon! Your support of the slave rebellion is unacceptable."

My blood boiled. The mission report had been challenging to read. Although I had not been one of the warriors undercover on that planet, their description of the atrocities committed there were enough to haunt me. It had been a long assignment, and only the blessing of my brathers finding their mates brought them back to the fold. If they hadn't, I feared the strain of their duty on Craxon might have pushed them into the depths of the void.

"From my understanding," I said evenly, showing none of the contempt I felt for this bastard, "it is already done. The people have won, and your Lords of Craxon are scattered to the wind."

His thin lips stretched into a sneer. "Do I look defeated, glack?"

The Craxion curse from his mouth did not bother me as much as his hand crawling toward his blaster. "I would not do that, your Lordship." I used his title as a warning, for it was clear to me he was one of the elite ruling class —the same that had fallen in the rebellion. "You will regret it."

"Will I?" Out of the crowd, two Oraders, insectoid aliens who were notorious for species trafficking, and two additional Craxions emerged. They took position next to the bastard and surrounded us. "I think not."

9

Jane

THIS IS GOING TO GET UGLY. GOOSEBUMPS ROSE ALONG my arms, the cool flesh a balm to my heated skin. In truth, I was itching for a fight. The Mangox had denied us earlier with his emergency call, and although fleeing was the wiser course of action, it didn't stop the adrenaline pumping through me.

I palmed Tor's dagger at my thigh. The hilt felt cool and right in my hand. It wasn't a blaster, but it would do the trick on these creepy-as-hell aliens. None of them were quite as tall as the commander, but the gray-skinned ones had claws and horns, while the bug guys had four arms and shells on their backs. Their mandibles twitched as the seconds ticked by.

"What's your end game, Craxion?" Tor asked, dropping his neutral tone of earlier, and opting for direct scorn. A silence permeated the space. The gray alien did not answer.

The breath before the battle was always the worst. It stretched onward to eternity while being no longer than a heartbeat. The bastards had surrounded us in a semi-circle, but Tor and I had already inched closer to each other. I knew without words when the fight broke out, I'd take the right two bug-men, and he'd take the left three gray-beasts. I wasn't quite sure how we'd communicated it to each other, and it was the most likely strategy given our positioning, but somehow, I sensed what Tor wanted.

Not something to think on now, Jane. Keep your head in the game. Squaring off with two aliens who had the size and weight advantage was not new to me—well, except for the alien part. *That* was new. But I practiced with the few remaining human males on Earth to become better at hand-to-hand combat. It might've been awhile, but I wasn't the moonbase captain for nothing.

"What ending do I want, glack?" The gray alien used that word again that didn't translate, but it didn't need to. His meaning was clear. "I want to see your blood pooling on the ground as the life leaves your worthless form."

"Poetic." Tor unsheathed his daggers, and I did the same. We kept our backs angled toward each other on a diagonal so as not to lose sight of our opponents. "But I'm afraid I don't plan on dying today."

The aliens spoke no more, but the leader reached for his blaster. Tor cut him off with a slice to his arm. The action broke loose the chains that had kept the fight at bay. I wasted no time in gaining ground on the bug-men. With their multiple arms and thick hides, I'd never gain purchase by staying on the outside. Like a beetle from Earth, I'd assessed their underbellies as the weak point, and I had to get past those swinging limbs to stand a chance.

My first strike hit the fleshy middle of bug alien one as I ducked under his flailing arms. He went down hard, curling his body into a ball and rolling on his shell. I didn't bother with him after, focusing on bug alien two. He'd observed my hit on his friend and warily stepped backwards while keeping me in his sights. Neither of the insectoids had blasters—or seemingly any weapons. But I wasn't going to be caught off-guard.

In my peripheral vision, I spotted Tor making short work of the gray-beasts. So far, none of them had gotten off a shot, despite outnumbering the commander. I smiled at his skill, but I didn't have the luxury of watching him fight as I had to defeat my other opponent.

"You should run now," I said to the bug-man. The ice in my voice would freeze most people, the insectoid was no exception. His mandibles locked in place, his antennas rising in two sharp lines above his head. "I won't give you a second warning."

The alien let loose a shrill shriek, and to my infinite shock, he whirled around and ran through the crowd. People parted a path for his departure. "Well, that's disappointing." I spun on my heel, making sure the first bug-man remained out for the count by stomping on his head. He slumped on his shell unconscious. While Tor had done a number on the gray aliens and knocked their blasters away, one tried to sneak attack him from behind. "Not on my watch."

I jumped in between the gray-beast and Tor's back. My dagger caught the bastard in the neck, but the weight of his fall meant the short sword between his hands sliced in a downward arc. The tip caught Tor's side and sliced a mean cut across his ribs.

"Damn it!" I screamed as the alien dropped his weapon and clutched his neck. He wasn't a threat anymore, but rage fired through me at the sight of the commander's wound. He didn't seem to feel it, however, as he bashed the skull of the final gray alien. I called to him, "Tor."

He turned to me, his eyes growing glassy as he did. A shudder went through him, and my strong warrior collapsed to one knee.

I screamed, "TOR!" My chest tightened as I caught him under the arms. He staggered in my grip, struggling to stay upright. "What is it? What's wrong?"

"Poison," he choked out. More of his weight fell to me. "Medpack."

"Right. Okay. It's going to be okay." Getting fully under him, I dragged his arm across my shoulders and heaved him up. "You have to hold on though. I need your help to get to the ship." He nodded and a fraction of his weight lifted. Together, we half shuffled, half staggered to our vessel. It wasn't far from the scene of our fight—thank the stars. But every step stretched out like a lifetime. Fear clenched my gut that we wouldn't make it, and I'd watch this strong, fearless warrior die before my eyes. *No. I won't let that happen. Damn it all.*

The aliens on the outpost gave us a wide berth. No one offered to help, but I had not expected them to. After seeing our fight, I doubted anyone would get involved, even if there was a half-decent alien on this stars-forsaken station.

When the ship came into view, I nearly slumped with relief. Tor groaned, little more than half-conscious by now. I put his palm to the ship's surface and the ramp lowered. As soon as we stepped onto the platform, I laid him on his back and programmed it to close. We had to get off the station, but his color was turning from that deep bronze hue to a pale taupe. I didn't have time to take off.

"Damn it." I paced the back of the ship for two steps. Then, I leaned over the commander and shook him awake. "Listen, cocky commander, you're not allowed to die on me. Now, where is the medpack?"

His gaze took stock of the room before landing on a lower section of the wall. "There," he rasped before his eyes closed, and he passed out.

"No." I dove for the wall. My nails dug into the paneling, searching for the medpack. When my finger slid around an arched section, I tore it free, and lo and behold, the elusive kit rested behind it. "Okay, okay. Come on."

I was no medic. In fact, whenever my mom was working, and I had to take my baby sisters for a checkup, I tended to invent all kinds of excuses. Until my mother grew wise to my ruse. *Honey, you have to face this fear sometime.* Her remembered words in my head brought tears to my eyes. "Well, mom, guess there's no time like the present."

I rifled through the pack. It had a ton of Rhonar words on it that I didn't understand. "Computer," I said, talking to the ship. "Which is the antidote for poison in the Rhonar medpack, and what do I do with it?"

"The proper procedure for poison is to identify the type." Before I could tell the computer that I didn't know the type, it continued, "If it cannot be identified use vial lorna as it has the widest range of properties."

I held up three vials. "Which one is correct? What does it look like?"

"Vial lorna is a blue bottle with clear liquid." The ship's artificial voice grounded me.

"Got it." I cupped it in my fist like a prize. "How do I administer it?"

"Open the stopper. Then, place the mouth of the vial, under the patient's tongue. Allow the contents to spread and encourage the patient to swallow." A bang against the side of the ship signaled we were running out of time—and had company.

I crawled on hands and knees over to Tor. His breathing was shallow, and panic snaked up my spine. I pushed it fiercely aside. *We do not have time for a freak out. I can do this.* Grabbing his mouth, I coaxed his lips apart. The top of the bottle was long and thin. I pulled the stopper free and tossed it aside. Slipping the tip into his mouth, I used my pointer finger to feel for his tongue. Unlike humans, he didn't have a mucus membrane to hold his tongue in place, so the vial slid easily underneath. Slowly, the contents spilled forth.

Another bang, louder and harder than the first, rocked the ship.

"Computer, initiate take off sequence." I had watched Tor pilot earlier. I might not be a medic, but I knew my way around a ship. And I loved to fly.

Hooking my hands under his armpits, I used all my strength to move him toward the wall. The back of the ship was not large, but it had thick bands attached to the walls to strap down cargo. Using one such band meant for a container, I looped it around his upper arms and chest, careful to avoid the cut on his ribs. It wasn't deep —the poison from it was the problem, not the cut itself —but it would have to be cleaned. *Later.* Another band around his thighs secured him in place. It wasn't a harness in the pilot's chair, but it would have to do.

With a last reluctant look at my alien warrior, I headed for the bridge. If I didn't get this ship moving, whoever was outside banging on the hull might ensure we didn't leave. And that was if the Mangox didn't find us first.

I strapped into the pilot's chair. My fingers flew over the console as I retrieved the coordinates for Sense VII. It occurred to me that we'd given the Mangox our real destination, and I feared we'd not seen the last of them. But the mission had to succeed. Whether the aliens followed us or not, we had to go to the planet and get the ergamite.

"Okay, launch sequence initiated." I grabbed the yoke and readied for take-off. "Three…two…one."

The ship shot through the energy dome above and cleared the outpost.

Through a series of trial and error where I almost blew the emergency hatch over my chair, I figured out how to employ stealth shielding. The commander had explained ships didn't fly with it engaged all the time because it drained the power quicker and forced more re-charging on their battle cruisers. But with the possibility of enemies coming after us, I thought it prudent. The Mangox might know our destination, but they did not need to pick us off in space.

With everything in order, I headed back to Tor. He laid where I left him, still asleep but his color was slowly returning, and his breathing evened. I sat beside him and drew his head gently into my lap. "What are you doing to me, cocky commander?" I sighed, stroking his thick black hair interspersed with silver strands. I had started to like the arrogant alien more than I cared to admit. He was brave, and strong, and surprisingly caring. He was a protector of his people, like me. It hit me that part of the reason we had such friction between us might be that we were more alike than not.

"I can't fall in love with you, Tor." My lungs constricted. I had experienced enough loss in life—first my parents, making me an orphan until my mother adopted me, then my best friend to a freak accident as a teen. And the incident with Sage, although my sister survived, had rattled me more than I let on. It was easier to keep walls around my heart than to let someone else in—and watch them die. "I don't want to lose anyone else."

TOR

The currents of the seas lapped against the pink sand shores. A voice carried on the breeze, beckoning me home. "Torian," my maether's cry matched the melody of the winds. "Time to eat."

I kicked the sand beneath my feet, racing across the beach to leap into her arms. She hugged me to her and spun in a circle. "My little adventurer." Laughing, she set me down and ruffled my hair. "What have you learned today?"

Chattering happily, I told her of all my findings. She listened with such care, although I'm sure my childish fascinations were of little matter to one of her station. As the chief scientist for Rhonar intelligence, she had far more important discoveries to make. Yet, she never made me feel like my explorations were any less valid.

As we talked and ate, the suns grew lower in the sky, casting shadows on the floor. Heavy steps sounded on our porch, when the door slid into the wall, revealing my paether. A honed and battle-hardened warrior, he led our fighters as their head commander. His leathers across his chest and legs were well-worn and in need of replacement. His katra, the markings on his arms, flowed from his shoulders to his wrists and glistened in the waning light of day.

I hopped off my chair. "Paether!"

He extended his arms wide and hoisted me in the air. "Greetings, young warrior." He smiled as he carried me back to my seat and set me in it. "Have you been good for your maether, today?"

"Of course, he has," she said with affection. "Here, I saved your dinner. Eat and regain your strength."

"Do you fear my strength ebbs, my Truxoria?" His gaze took in my maether, a deep love evident in his stormy gray eyes.

She bent beside him and whispered something in his ear that made him chuckle. Wrapping his hand around the back of her neck, he kissed her for several beats, then pulling away he said, "I look forward to showing you."

My child's mind was mesmerized by the interaction. I soaked it up like a sea-sponge, absorbing the scene into my memory. Even then, I knew how special such times were. But as I was so young, long before the first biological stage consumed me with the hunger, my thoughts never stayed on one matter too long. "Paether, will you tell me about the war?"

I was driven by the news of the war with our most fearsome enemy. Not being old enough for fighting, and barely allowed to train with more than wooden weapons, I yearned to learn more of battle. My maether wanted me to become a scientist like her, but the call of the warrior was too much to resist.

"For that, we must walk, Torian." He rose from his chair and held out a hand to me. "Come." His callused fingers wrapped around my smooth palm and tugged me to the door. "We will be back soon, my mate."

"Be well, my loves." She waved as we took the steps off the porch and onto the sands.

For several clicks, we simply walked. When we reached the edge of the seas where the cliff met the water, he turned to me and placed our hands together, palm to palm. "Do you see how my hand is larger than yours?"

"Yes, Paether." I watched as he curled his fingers, encompassing mine completely in his.

"That is how the hunger works on us. It claims us in its hold." He held tighter. The grip was not painful but uncomfortable. "Do you feel how you want to break free of it?"

I nodded. The sensation of needing to tear my hand away grew stronger with every beat.

He let go. "The void takes over next. A sensation of loss like none which I can describe to you. It is beyond words." A faraway look grew in his eyes as if he recalled the time before he'd found my maether, his mate. "I pity such males lost in the emptiness."

"I know about our biology. We learned in training." I bounced on the balls of my feet, dismissing my paether's solemn words. "What about the war?"

"It's all a part of it, Torian." He sighed and knelt to meet me at eye level. "The Versaken are not as different from us as we'd like to fool ourselves." A tick formed in his jaw before he shook his head as if to banish the heavy thoughts. "But you, my child, are a warrior-born. One day you may well lead." He placed a dagger in my hand, the first of many I'd gather in my life. "You must be prepared that for every victory, you will have an equal failure. You will lose people, even those you love." He pushed my fingers to curl around the hilt. "But no matter the hardships you endure," the dying light glinted off the metal, "you must never lose yourself."

10

Jane

THE HOURS DRONED ON. AFTER USING COMPONENTS from the medpack, I'd sealed the cut on Tor's ribs and bandaged the wound. I'd paced for a while, ate a snack from the kitchens, changed into a tank-top and sweatpants, checked the coordinates three times, programmed the computer to monitor the space around us, and disengaged the stealth shielding once far enough from the Mangox outpost to conserve power.

When nothing was left to do, I returned to monitor Tor's condition. He slept like the dead, and it freaked me the fuck out. To try and ease the fear slithering through me like an insidious snake, I sat with my back to the wall and his head in my lap. I reasoned that I could keep him with me, if I just held onto him. It was delusional, but I didn't care.

I must have nodded off at some point as I awoke to the sound of the computer beeping. "Destination in ten clicks."

I rubbed the sleep from my eyes and stretched my arms overhead. It took me a minute to realize I wasn't in the back of the ship. A soft mattress laid under me, a cool sheet over me. I sprang from the bed and ran toward the bridge. There, in the pilot's chair, sat Tor. His hands rested on the ship's yoke.

I swallowed the lump in my throat. "Tor?"

He rose at the sound of my voice and turned toward me. The bandage was gone from his side and all that remained of the injury was a faint white line against his bronze skin. "Fair meet, Jane."

My eyes filled with tears as he spoke the formal Rhonar greeting. A wave of anger crashed over me, warring with my relief that he lived. I slapped my hands against his chest, once, twice, again and again. "You almost died." Fear like I hadn't experienced since that day when my sister was blown into space had been dogging my steps from the moment Tor fell. I hadn't noticed it until now, but his near-death experience had eaten away at my resolve. No matter what my mind said, my heart knew the truth. I was falling in love with the commander. And I'd come so close to losing him. "Why weren't you more careful?"

He stilled my strikes by capturing my hands against his chest. He held them there, my palms against his pecs. His double hearts beat beneath my touch. "I am sorry, my Truxoria." His lips brushed my cheeks, kissing away the tears. "I never meant to cause you pain."

"I wasn't the one hurt." I jerked back from his hold to narrow my eyes at him. "You were."

A smirk tugged at his lips. "I was. But I had my new Terran hero to save me."

"No." I wagged a finger in his face. "I am not getting another nickname. You hear me?"

"Yes, my ljona." His lips found my forehead, my temple, and my cheeks once more. "You are right."

When his mouth found mine, his tongue plunged inside. The whirlwind of emotions shifted to instant heat at his touch. I wanted to yell at him more. I hated feeling afraid and preferred to express it with anger, but the building inferno inside me didn't care what I wanted.

I moaned into his mouth.

"One click to destination." The computer's message broke us apart.

Panting, I stared into his eyes, not sure what I was seeking beyond the lust that swam through me. But his purple rimmed eyes glowed with silver. The emotions in that gaze were more than mere desire. I had the urge to wrap my legs around him and beg him to take me while simultaneously needing to run away as far and fast as I could. He must have seen something in my face as he snagged a hand in my hair and tilted my head back. He ran his clever tongue up the side of my neck, then kissed me once more before letting me go.

"Computer," he said, reclaiming his spot in the pilot's chair. "Inform the hosts of our arrival and prepare for landing."

I wobbled on my feet before gaining my bearings. I plopped into the co-pilot's chair and strapped in. The screen displayed a small golden planet with one sun. The land masses glistened as if alight from within. Patches of purple water were splattered across the surface. "It's beautiful."

Tor turned to me, a soft expression on that strong, chiseled face. "Yes, I agree."

A flush warmed my neck. By the open admiration in his eyes, I knew he wasn't talking about the planet.

"Greetings, visitors!" A feminine voice called as the screen shifted. An alien with enormous eyes, like an anime character, small nose, and bow shaped mouth appeared. Long golden hair flowed from her forehead and around pointed ears. Her skin was a pale-yellow shade like the petals of a tulip. "I am Calia, mate of Lorn. We're happy to welcome you to Sense VII."

"Thank you for your welcome. I am Torian, Commander of the Rhonar." He bowed his head and rested his fist on his sternum. Then, he waved at me. "This is my partner, Captain Jane Kadaran of Earth."

"Wonderful!" The alien named Calia gave a one-handed clap. "It is our honor to have you to our planet. Please direct your ship to the landing bay at the Prism

Palace." Her image winked out as a map replaced it on the screen with distinctive coordinates. "We'll meet you there."

Tor closed the com while I programmed the ship to the given directions. His brows winged up as his gaze followed my hands. "You weren't lying when you said you'd learn how to fly the ship in a short time." He shot me a half-smile. "I still can't believe how much you picked up. Took me forever to learn to pilot."

"It's my gift." I waved it off as if it were of no consequence. But inside, I was dancing. I'd always been a sucker for compliments, but his praise gave me a whole other level of contentment.

"It's more than that." He handed me a holo-pad attached to the console. "But let's prep for the meeting. You read about the Kinsians in the mission research."

"Yes." I nodded and swiped to the section on Kinsians. "They're a species who are addicted to," I cleared my throat, "sensual pleasure and knowledge of the universe. They possess vast records of galactic history and alien biology on their home world." My eyes skipped over the paragraph describing their planet. "They're born with white or gray pigment to their skin, but it alters when they mate to form complimentary colors or shades of the same hue." I cocked my head to the side as I read. "That's neat. One mate for life. Yada-yada. Where's the stuff on Sense VII?"

"It's further down." He motioned to his holo-pad where he had it opened and read, "They created a colony on the small planet to serve 'all those who seek knowledge' as is their motto."

"And it just so happens, the planet they chose houses some of the rarest materials in the universe." I scoffed.

He shrugged as the ship landed. "As you can imagine with all the knowledge they've acquired," he undid his harness and rose, "they are not a stupid people."

I matched his steps as we headed toward the back of the ship. "Are they going to help us is the question?"

"My brathers met a mated Kinsian pair during the rebellion I told you about before."

I shivered as I thought about those gray-beasts and bug-men. They were officially on my shit-list for almost killing Tor. "What side were they on?"

The ramp opened, and we headed planet-side. Tor took my hand in his as we descended. "The couple aided my brathers for many cycles and helped the rebels." He patted his daggers beneath his vest with his free hand. "Still, don't let your guard down."

"Didn't plan on it." I rolled my shoulders, preparing for our mission. "But that's some comfort."

I'd studied the details of the planet, but I was not prepared for the sight before us. The Prism Palace was aptly named with soaring towers that refracted the light of the enormous orange sun. Rainbows danced between the towers as if they were living beings, dancing on the winds.

"It's incredible." I breathed deeply, the scents of jasmine and lavender floating on the air.

An alien couple bounded toward us, the pale-yellow Calia of earlier, and a banana-hued larger person next to her. The taller one had copper hair but the same huge, rounded eyes. When they reached us, Calia spoke, "Allow me to introduce Lorn, my mate."

"Greetings, travelers. It's a pleasure to have new guests." His voice was an octave deeper than his partner, and he had a more angular bone structure, but in every other facet of their appearance they matched. Even their clothes, which consisted of flowing dark green tunics and pants, complimented one another.

"Thank you," Tor bowed once more. "Jane and I are humbled by your welcome. We are in search of a rare item that will aid our peoples, and we hope you will help us in procuring it."

I hid a smile behind my hand, pretending to scratch my nose. Tor's all-business, direct approach was so like the bossy commander I'd first met. But in our shared time together, I'd seen a whole other side of him. *And I think I like both.* Warmth suffused me at the thought.

"Of course. The Rhonar are an honorable people." Calia's bow mouth created a heart-shape when she smiled. "We are happy to be of service."

"That is most kind of you, indeed." Tor placed his fist to his sternum, an action that showed the highest form of respect for the Rhonar. "We seek ergamite."

Lorn waved us to walk on the path leading to the palace. Golden in color with square blocks, it reminded me of a fictional road from a storybook, but I couldn't remember which. "Now, Commander," the Kinsian male began, striding beside his mate, "you must understand that we will help you in any way we can, but we have strict rules when it comes to those who seek at our sanctum."

"But it's not for us alone that we've come," I interjected. The research I studied had shown Kinsians craved knowledge—and sensual pleasures, but I couldn't see how that was relevant in this situation. But they also regarded the lives of all species as most sacred. "The ergamite ensures the safety of our peoples. It's for our very survival."

I might have been stretching the truth a tad. But if we didn't get the ergamite, then our negotiations would fall apart. A ripple effect that could easily lead to the downfall of both Rhonar and humans alike.

Calia patted my free hand as she walked on my left. "Do not fear, Captain Jane. You will have the chance to earn what you need."

"Earn?" Tor asked. He held my other hand and squeezed it gently in silent warning.

"Yes." She clapped both hands together this time and let free a high-pitched squeal. "Oh, it's splendid! It's been so long since we've had a couple seeking at our door. I am sure the fates will choose well for your tests!"

I blinked. Had I heard that right?

Tor beat me to the question. "What tests do you mean?"

"You must wait and discover what the stars have in store." The Kinsian female's enigmatic answer was of little comfort. But it drew an end to the conversation as we arrived at a set of double doors, marking the entrance of the palace. The door panels stood like two giant sentinels with deep symbols carved into their diamond-like surface. Calia held her arms extended out and said, "Amiara."

The doors swung open, revealing a golden carpet draped over a stone black floor. The path of golden bricks matched perfectly with the interior carpet, so that only the doorway marked where one ended and the other began. The effect created an endless line that linked the outer world with the inner. I noted this absently as we walked, and Calia picked up the thread of my thoughts.

"Marvelous, is it not?" She asked me when we headed inside. "The way our outer and inner lives are brought together."

"It is," I agreed readily, wanting these aliens on our side for whatever was to come. "Did your people create all this?"

"Not exactly," Lorn chimed in. "It is more accurate to say we formed it out of the universe's desires."

Tor did a poor job of covering a skeptical vocalization with a cough.

I side-eyed him as we continued the trek into the palace. "How do you know what the universe wants?" I asked in a more neutral tone.

"Well, my Earth friend." The Kinsian male grabbed a handful of dust from a side bowl and threw it high above his head. The fragments scattered on a light breeze, creating glittering light wherever they landed and illuminating our path forward. "The wishes of the stars are all around you. You have but to look for them."

Not knowing how to respond, I chose silence as the wisest course.

"Here we are." Calia stopped in front of a side door that appeared no different than the rest that lined the hall. "You may cleanse and change here, Captain Jane." She pointed to another door next to the first. "And you here, Commander Torian."

"Please, call me Jane," I said automatically as she used my title for a second time. Then, the other part of her sentence hit me. "Cleanse and change how?"

Calia laughed, a tinkling sound like rain on tin. "Your bodies and clothes, of course. You cannot undergo the trials in that." She pointed to my clothes first, then Tor's. Her round eyes narrowed, looking like squished melons.

"And no weapons. They are strictly forbidden in the sanctum."

I shot Tor a look that he'd understand without words. He shook his head side-to-side slowly, just enough for me to notice. "We will do all that is required, my friends." Tor shirked off his vest and handed it to Lorn. "All of my weapons reside in there."

Calia waited, staring expectantly at me.

I sighed. Removing the dagger and its sheath Tor had given me from my pants, I handed it to her. "Please don't lose it." I cast a glance at my alien warrior. "It's special to me."

"Your things will all be safe. I can assure you." She took it from my hand, holding it in hers like it was a sacred treasure. Her care made me feel a fraction better about turning over the dagger. "Now, please head into your cleansing and changing areas. The units will refresh your bodies and clothes have already been prepared for you."

"That's," Tor scrunched his face as if he wanted to argue, but he straightened it quickly as he said, "kind of you."

"It is no trouble at all." Lorn folded the vest carefully over his arm. "When you've finished, the interior door will lead you to our dining hall. We've had a meal prepared for you as well, so you may nourish yourselves before your trials begin."

"That is truly kind of you," I said, meaning the words. We may not know what laid in store for us with these tests, but I couldn't fault the Kinsians on their hospitality.

"We love having seekers." Mirth danced in Calia's round eyes. "It invigorates our spirits and renews our souls. Does it not, my Lorn?"

"It does, indeed." The Kinsian couple locked eyes, and it was clear that love flowed between them. Love and…a lot more.

"Well," I cleared my throat, hoping to break up the eye-fucking between the alien pair, "Tor and I will just get ourselves settled, then come and meet you."

The Kinsians didn't acknowledge us, or even blink as their weird staring contest continued.

Tor bent to speak in my ear. "I think we'd better just go and let them," he raised one brow as the couple began to emit odd squeals, "do whatever they're doing."

"Good idea." I headed quickly for my door while Tor claimed his. "Meet you on the other side."

He paused and leaned toward me once more. His lips brushed my mouth in a soft kiss. "Be safe, Jane." His growl rolled along my insides, setting them aflame. "I don't like leaving you."

"I'll be fine." I tweaked his nose. "Go freshen up, bossy alien."

He bit my finger gently. "Behave, little captain, or you will be punished."

My eyes widened. Before I could respond with an appropriate comeback, he disappeared behind his door.

"Cocky, arrogant, son of a viper!" I shrieked after his retreating form.

He didn't respond, but his bark of laughter stayed behind.

11

Tor

My skin itched under the gauzy fabric. Now, I knew how Jane felt when she'd worn her... *What did she call it? Lin-ray? Lana-drey?* Well, whatever it was called, it had to be comparable to this bizarre outfit.

Using the cleanser had been a simple enough affair. It was a light-based unit that cleaned the skin, hair, and nails in an efficient fashion. But the clothes had been another matter. The shoes were plain soles that wrapped around the feet with straps. The white cloth had an iridescent sheen to it and wrapped diagonal around the torso and chest. Then, it hung loose at the waist like a gladiator style garb. I hadn't fought in the galactic games, but the fighters who did wore a similar style.

"Although, it was not constructed of this lightweight material." I squished the fabric between my thumb and forefinger. Sure enough, it was see-through in the right light. *Well, that'll be interesting.*

Feeling like a pruned and plucked sao-sao bird, I headed for the dining hall. The short time away from Jane already had me aching to see her again. The closer we got to completing this mission, the greater my desire grew to make her mine.

"Are you as uncomfortable as I am?" Jane stood in her outfit like a celestial goddess. The fabric complemented her coloring as the light reflected off her skin and cast rainbows across her body. Her tight curls had softened into looser ringlets, thanks to the cleanser, and it shone with vibrancy. The material was crisscrossed over her breasts and then hung in a similar fashion to mine about her waist.

"You look beautiful," I said in earnest.

"Thank you." She sighed, pulling at the cloth and stretching it from her body. "But it's not my style."

I chuckled and snatched her hand from the fabric. "I feel the same, but it does not change the truth. It suits you."

Her gaze traveled my body, as if seeing me for the first time. Her breath hitched. "You don't look so bad yourself."

"Ah, you two appear refreshed." Calia's voice broke up our momentary reverie. She waved us to a round table in the center of the dining hall. "Come let us give you nourishment, so you may begin your trials."

The table was a rustic wood design with a star carved in the middle. Floating orbs illuminated the room in soft amber hues. A mix of savory and sweet smells wafted from the delicious looking feast spread on a cart beside Lorn's chair. He picked up each dish, placed it on the table, and bade us sit. "Eat and drink as you wish, dear friends. If you crave a certain flavor, you have but to think it, and the food will adjust to your tastes."

"The food can change?" Jane sat in the chair across from the Kinsian female, while I claimed the seat in between.

"In a manner of speaking." Passing a plate stacked with meats and vegetables, Calia explained the process. "In this room, we can manifest our desire for sustenance. So, the food doesn't alter from its natural state, but our perception of it shifts."

Jane poked at the pile of meat. "I've never heard of anything like that, but I'll give it a try." She took one piece with her thumb and forefinger. "Here goes." Plopping it in her mouth, her eyes widened as she chewed. "That tastes just like the steaks my mom used to grill for us on summer holiday."

Her experience had me curious to test it for myself. I grabbed a cubed chunk and imagined my paether's Palaxian stew. When I put it in my mouth and bit down, I was not prepared for the intense emotion that flooded me along with the flavor. It was like walking on the sands with my paether again as we talked in a different time. I could almost hear my maether calling me. Remnants of the dream-memory emerged as I chewed. Sweat beaded on my neck and rolled down my chest.

"Tor," a voice summoned me, but it sounded so far away. "Hey, cocky commander, come back."

Jane? The past and present merged until I swallowed the food. I hadn't remembered closing my eyes, but I opened them again to stare into Jane's concerned face. "My ljona."

"Are you with us?" She snapped her fingers at me.

I shot her a half-grin. "I think so."

"Don't do that again," she chided and swiped my plate from me. Gathering the meat, she plunked it on her plate, then piled her vegetables on mine and handed it back. "All veggies for you this meal."

I laughed, a deep sound from the gut that caught me off-guard. When had I laughed, *truly* laughed before? My mate was a wonder like none in this universe. I needed to claim her soon before I went mad with longing.

"Come on," she said, waving at the pile of veggies she'd given me. "Eat up, but think about something pleasant, okay? No weird zoning out."

"Yes, little captain." I waggled my brows at her. "I'll do my best."

The Kinsians observed our encounter with equal mirth, and the conversation flowed freely. The pair had no reservations in showing their affection for each other.

Simple touches on the hand or long stares, which admittedly Jane and I both found a bit odd, occurred throughout the meal. Despite their different mannerisms, I enjoyed their company, and I found myself desiring a similar rapport with my mate as the couple had with one another.

"Thank you for a fine meal." I rose to help Lorn place the dishes back on the tray.

Calia nodded. "You are most welcome. Would you like to begin the tests now, or would you prefer to rest first?"

I turned to Jane for her answer. I'd been unconscious for most of the ride here, albeit not of my choosing, and I was ready to face the trials. But I didn't know how much sleep my brave ljona had gotten while tending to me. "Jane?"

Rising from her seat, she flexed her bicep and slapped the muscle. "I'm set."

Pride surged through me at her resolve. Her first trip into deep space had been a difficult journey, and our mission had only begun as we prepared for the trials. Yet, she faced any challenge head on without complaint. I did not believe I was worthy of such a mate, but I could not deny that the universe had chosen well. No other would be as perfect for me as her.

"May the stars be with you." Lorn waved to us as he wheeled the food cart away. "Calia will tell you about the first test and lead you to it. I will see you again for the second."

"Thank you." I bowed my head as he disappeared through a rear corridor.

"Now then," Calia said as she led us through an arched doorway and to the main hall with its golden carpet. "The first test is often physical." The construction of the palace in its prism design created an optical illusion, as if the hall and its rich rug spread off into infinity. "With a pairing such as yours," she motioned to where Jane and I had linked hands again, "I don't think you'll have trouble, but do not hold back."

"We'll give it our all." Jane tilted her chin and held her head high. "We will succeed."

I squeezed her hand in mine. "We will."

"I have no doubt." Calia stopped in front of a diamond shaped door. The tip at the top was painted ruby red while the rest of it bore a midnight black hue. "You'll sense what you need to do." A watery smile tugged at her lips. I may have been new to emotions, but I could read the hope for us in her face. Her obvious caring toward us humbled me. "May the fates guide you."

The door slid open at her words, revealing a room of solid darkness. No light penetrated the space.

"In there?" Jane said, a ring of doubt circling her question.

"Yes," Calia said as she stepped back from the entrance. "You can do this. Remember, don't hold back." With that, she left us at the threshold to our first trial.

My ljona gulped. "No time like the present as they say?"

"Wait." I dropped her hand and put my arms around her. I drew her to my chest, her head resting above my hearts. "We'll be all right, Jane. I won't let anything happen to you."

She snorted and leaned back. "Well, maybe *I* won't let anything happen to *you*, since you seem to be the one getting yourself hurt and all."

"Brave, little captain." I pinched her nose.

She swatted my hand away, laughing as she did. "Cocky commander."

My cock hardened, threatening to show through the sheer fabric. "I told you I liked when you called me that." I pulled her flush against me, letting her feel my desire.

"Maybe I remembered." Her voice turned husky, and a hint of her arousal reached my nose.

"Jane," I warned, not having the time to take her as I desperately wanted.

Running a light touch around my ribs, she said, "Just don't get hurt again. I don't like it."

"Yes, Captain." I brought her fingers to my mouth and kissed each one. "As you say."

We turned as one to enter the first test. With the room as dark as it was, even I struggled to see. Jane kept a death grip on my arm. We walked forward, each step heavy and solid before proceeding to the next.

"I can't see a thing in here." Her voice was strained. "I wish we had some light." As if in response to her request, a bright silvery ray streamed from above. It shone like a moonbeam casting an ethereal glow. Jane stretched out her hand, wiggling her fingers in the light, and let free a heavy sigh. "That's better."

Before I could decipher the meaning of this light and darkness, a force swept us off our feet. We floated in midair as if the gravity had been eliminated from the room.

"Tor," Jane laid suspended in the middle of the glowing moonbeam, "what's going on?"

"Zero gravity," I hypothesized from our situation.

"Yeah, but why?" Her gauzy outfit turned translucent under the silvery light.

My hearts beat faster as I watched her, the mating bond calling louder than ever in my soul. I breathed her name, "Jane."

Her gaze slid to me, a question in those shining blue eyes. "Tor?"

A sense of knowing washed through me. I needed to pleasure my mate, to prove I'd satisfy her need. Even a lack of gravity would not stop me. "I'm going to make you come, Jane."

Her mouth fell open. "But we have to figure out…" Her nose scrunched. "…ah the…" Understanding gleamed in her eyes. "It's a test of desire?"

"The Kinsians told us we'd be suited for the task." I stretched my toes toward the wall and grazed it with the sole of the sandal, but in the zero-gravity environment it was enough to propel me toward my mate. When I glided to the center of the moonbeam, I grabbed her leg and spun to stop my progress. We floated together under the glow. "And Calia did mention a physical task."

"Yeah," she flung her arms up, which sliced slowly through the empty air, "but I thought it'd be like fighting, or skills test, or something."

A knowing smile tugged at the corner of my lip. "I think the skill test theory applies."

She shot me a withering glare. "You are not helping."

"Don't worry, my fierce ljona," I grasped around her waist and tugged her to me, "I will." The zero-gravity meant faster movements were impossible without using the walls to propel us. Not wanting to bounce around like a zoolat in a cage, I opted for the slower pace. Trying to claim her like this would be futile, but that didn't mean I was incapable of pleasing my Truxoria.

Cradling her head in one hand and using the other around her waist to anchor her to me, I began a long, leisurely exploration of her mouth. My tongue delved inside, coaxing hers to dance with mine. Her hands gripped my arms, nails digging into my skin. Our legs tangled together. When we broke apart, her breaths grew rapid. I wasted no time in licking along the sensitive skin at her neck, laving it with attention and finding the spots that made her moan. Her hips rocked, seeking relief.

"I need more," she cried.

"And you shall have it." With my cock harder than I'd been in my life, I wanted to bury it deep in my mate. But the lack of gravity meant my desire would have to wait. I grasped her seeking hips and slowly pulled her up. The motion put my head in line with her breasts. "Ah," I said, admiring the sheer fabric perfectly outlining her hard peaks. "I must have a taste."

Ducking my head, I ran my tongue around the enticing tip, the fabric becoming wet as I did so. Her hands found my hair and tugged. I loved the sting of it as I brought that beautiful breast into my mouth and sucked hard.

"Tor!" she screamed, and the sound was better than any music. I licked the sides of her breasts, the creamy slopes, and drew circles around the beautiful peaks. Enjoying every beat of pleasure I pulled from my Jane. Sucking and licking in equal measures, she soon begged for my touch. "Please, I can't take much more."

Her legs shifted restlessly, despite the zero-gravity restricting the pace. I needed her on my tongue, to taste my mate again. I'd never get enough of her flavor. Using my body as a counterbalance, I shifted her further up.

When my face was in line with her wet pussy, I pushed the gauzy fabric aside, so I could lap at her sweet folds. Her clit poked from its hood, desperate for attention. I gently laid my lips over it and sucked. Her fingers bit into my scalp.

"Oh stars, fuck!" Her cries grew urgent. "It's so good."

I speared her on my tongue, letting it vibrate inside her core. Then, I ran the tip of it along that tender spot inside her again and again. When her pants and cries grew to a crescendo, I replaced my tongue with two long fingers and thrust to the hilt. I did this over and over while using my tongue to vibrate against her clit. When her inner walls began to spasm, I clamped down on her throbbing clit and sucked.

"Yes!" Her screams rent the air, echoing off the walls.

As her body shook with the aftershocks of her climax, I licked her through it. When she came back down, we too floated to the floor. She sagged in my arms, her legs not yet holding her weight. I kept her steady, while she regained her bearings. Her hands gripped my waist.

As we stood in each other's embrace, the moonbeam from above spread over the space, until the room was encapsulated in glowing silver light. The diamond door opened with Lorn standing on the other side.

"Well done," he did his one-handed clap. "You've passed the first test."

Jane's spine straightened and her brows winged toward her hairline. Her words sputtered forth on a hard gasp. "Were you watching us?"

"Watching?" Lorn tilted his head to the side. "Certainly not. The seeker tests are a private matter. We'd never dream of intruding."

"Oh, good." She flapped a hand in the air, using the other to rearrange her outfit. "I mean, that's good to know."

"I'm glad you have passed the first test." The Kinsian's smile appeared kind yet knowing. The couple might not watch, but I had a feeling they knew exactly what these tests were about. They did host the trials after all. "Onward to the next. Are you both ready?"

My ljona ran her gaze over my body, taking a pause at my cock hidden behind the gauzy fabric. "But you didn't...ah..."

Chuckling low, I took her hand in mine. "It's all right, little captain. I'm looking forward to continuing our endeavors, later." I motioned toward the Kinsian. "Lead on, Lorn. We're ready."

"Excellent." He led us into the hall, and our mission continued.

I kept my focus on Jane. No matter what we faced, we would do it together, and I'd keep my ljona safe. But despite my resolve, I couldn't help but wonder, *What will be next?*

12

Jane

WHAT COULD POSSIBLY BE NEXT? I THOUGHT AS WE walked down the endless hallway. So many doors lined each side of the corridor, all with different shapes, colors, and designs. I stuck close to Tor, enjoying the feel of his larger hand in mine. As my curiosity grew, I gave voice to my most pressing question. "Lorn, are all the tests the same?"

"Oh no." Lorn cast a glance over his shoulder at me. "They're tailored to the needs of the seekers."

Tor caught on to my wavelength, asking, "Who designs the tests?"

"Well," the Kinsian looked straight ahead once more, but continued talking as we walked, "it's a combination of factors. My people built the Prism Palace to be intuitive. It's not sentient, but it can sense the needs of the seekers who join us here." He stopped before a circular door constructed of a gleaming gold metal. "The original architects programmed the palace to test the seekers in three distinct trials relevant to themselves and the knowledge they seek. Calia and I host the visitors."

A knot formed in the pit of my stomach. "What if a person fails the trials?"

"Then, I'm afraid they are unable to claim what they seek." Lorn pushed open the golden door to reveal a vast forest. "But I am confident in your pairing. Go and be of true voice."

His cryptic parting message had my eyes narrowing as I passed him and entered the room. Trees and flowers of every shape and color surrounded a field in the center. It reminded me of the first room in its circular shape. Yet, where the first was empty, this place was packed to overflowing. Everywhere I looked plants bloomed, stretching their petals toward the golden light that streamed from an artificial sky.

"Calia will meet you for test three." With that, Lorn shut the door behind us.

I shot Tor a cheeky grin. "So, you any good at gardening?"

He snorted. "Somehow I doubt that's the test."

I laughed. "Probably not."

Heading to the center of the room as we had with the first test, we walked into a circular field of blue grass. It was the only spot that had any open area, the rest of the room being covered in an array of flowers and trees. Around the edge of the circle, gray, furry plants lined the perimeter. About as big as my head, they appeared like soft rocks, shaping the field. We stepped over the nearest one, careful not to disturb it as we did so.

The sunlight warmed my skin. I spun around, enjoying the feel of it while also remaining vigilant for hints of our trial. I stopped my twirls and tucked my fist under my chin. "Any ideas?"

"Nothing yet." He tapped his foot on the soft grass, clearly as anxious as I to get through these trials. "I had a sense of knowing what to do before, an intuition, I suppose." He scrubbed his hand over his neck. "But there's nothing like that now."

"Yeah," I drew out the word, distracted by a slight rocking on the edge of the field. I wasn't sure if it were an optical illusion or a problem with my eyes, but the furry rocks appeared to be swaying. I grabbed the hem of his outfit and tugged. "Tor, are you seeing this?"

As if on cue, the furry rocks, which apparently were not rocks at all, floated off the ground until they reached about my eye level. Then, they cracked open!

"What the—?" Tor's question mirrored mine, but we didn't have time to react.

From their split centers vines shot forward faster than a snake strike. Blue slithering vines as thick as my wrist wrapped around us. The largest circled our waists, hoisting Tor and I into the air, while the rest held our arms and legs in an X shape.

I screamed. Snakes were a secret fear of mine, not having even told my sisters about it, and these vines reminded me way too much of the slimy creatures. "Fuck. Shit. I can't move."

"Calm down, Ijona. You're breathing too fast." Tor was held equally captive by the vines, but he wasn't panicking like me.

"I can't. This freaks me out." Tears sprang to my eyes, and I couldn't control a sob that wracked my body. "Can you get loose?"

He flexed and pulled hard, the muscles in his biceps straining. "It's no use. They're bound too tight."

The vines had gone taut, holding us in place. It helped ease the fear slithering through me, but I was not anywhere near chill about our situation. "We need to get free."

"Agreed." Tor strained again, managing to budge the vine on his right wrist a fraction. "These crexers are strong."

Okay, relax. Breathe. You can do this. I closed my eyes and imagined the vines loosening their hold. The Kinsians said the palace reacted on the needs of the seekers. And I needed these damn vines off me. I opened my eyes to find we were still suspended by the creepy bastards. Panic rose in my throat. "Nothing's working."

"Jane." His firm use of my name had me turning my gaze to his. He was bound directly across from me, no more than two arms' lengths away. Out of reach, but near enough to see the fire in his eyes. "Breathe in and out through your nose. Count to twelve. And then, tell me what's wrong."

"Besides being captured by creepy vines?" My snarky attitude wrapped around me like armor.

"Yes," he said patiently, no longer battling the vines but focusing his attention exclusively on me. "Besides that."

A tugging sensation in my chest compelled me to do as he said. I took in a few breaths, the air sawing in and out my nose. I counted up to twelve and back again. Then, I met his intense stare. "I'm afraid of snakes." The truth soared from me like a space fighter launching into orbit. "When I was five, my parents, my biological ones I mean, took me hiking. Earth doesn't have many spots left for that sort of thing, but they loved nature. Any chance they could they'd show me all the plants and wildlife the planet had to offer."

Tears stung the back of my eyes as the precious memory of my parents collided with what happened next. "We were walking up a hill, and I was getting tired. My dad picked me up and carried me, while my mom went ahead to scout us an easy trail back." I sucked in a ragged breath. "I was sleepy and whiny, and he was more focused on me and my needs, so he didn't see the snake crossing the path. It struck him in the leg."

"Jane," my alien's voice grounded me in the present, giving me the strength to carry on. "You are with me, my Truxoria. You are safe."

"It didn't kill him. My mom came running at my screams and gave him an antidote." I shuddered at the memory. "But neither of them was the same after that. And it's stuck with me too."

"They sound like wonderful parents." His tone was filled with empathy, but something more too.

I nodded. "They were. I love my adopted mom. She's my mother as much as my first. I'm lucky to have gotten three amazing parents in my lifetime." My heart skipped a beat. "It's still hard. And the things I went through after they passed, before my second mother adopted me were…" I didn't want to dive into that dark hole, the traumas were wounds that never healed. But I wasn't that child locked in her room anymore. I was an adult and I'd live for today. "Well, I don't want to get into that." I shook my head. "The good outweighs the bad. Even though my parents died when I was young, I remember everyday with them."

"I'm glad you've had these people in your life, my ljona." His chin fell to his chest as his face took on a distant look. "And I am sorry that you've suffered. I understand your pain."

My gaze found his. "Tell me."

"You know the Versaken's biological attack killed all of our females, yes?" He asked the question like the commander he was, as if giving a report—and detaching from the emotions.

I couldn't imagine what it would be like to lose all emotions, and then, suddenly regain them all at once. It must be overwhelming. It made me wonder how Tor would handle such a thing…and if he already was. But I did not voice my suspicions. It was his turn to speak his truth. "Yes," I said in answer. "Go on."

"The attack claimed my maether's life," he paused, turning away from me for a second, "slowly. She didn't die right away."

I gasped. "Tor, I'm so sorry."

"Thank you. It was…" Another pause as he took a breath. "It was the hardest thing I've ever endured. For my paether, it was unbearable. He stayed alive to guide me into malehood, but after that, he put himself on suicide missions. Always seeking the enemy, until the enemy found him."

"By the universe." I yearned to break free of these stupid vines and hold him. "There's no words. But I'm here. I'm here with you."

"I know, my Truxoria. I know." Our eyes locked. As if we could hold each other, his gaze stroked my body like a caress. "And I'm ready to tell you what that word means, if you'd still like to know."

A part of me already knew the answer. I'd felt it since the moment we met, staring at his chiseled jaw and intense eyes through a screen. Even when he drove me insane with his arrogance, I sensed a deeper part locked inside him. As I saw it emerge the longer I was in his company, I realized that he wasn't the cocky commander I'd thought. He was confident and caring, strong and empathetic, because he felt. He felt everything. He had emotions, and that could only mean one thing. "Say it."

"Truxoria is the most scared word in our language, equal only to our name for the universal goddess, Celestia." His head bowed in reverence as he spoke. When he looked up and captured my gaze, his eyes glistened silver. "It means fated mate, and you, Jane…" His words skimmed over my skin, sinking deep into my chest, and wrapping around my heart. "You are mine."

The vines began to unravel, easing from our limbs and bringing us back to the blue field. When they released us, we ran to each other. I jumped into his arms as he caught me to his chest.

"I knew it," I said, the rightness of it seeping into my soul. "I somehow knew it all along."

He kissed my temple, smiling the biggest I'd seen from him yet. "My wise mate."

I laughed, and the sunshine on our bodies warmed my insides. Or maybe it was his body heat. With our shared pasts laid bare and our fates aligned, I wanted one thing above all others, even more than completing the mission. "I want you, Tor." I bit his earlobe, then looked in his eyes so he could see the full truth of my confession. "Make me yours."

The idea of someone claiming me in the past would have sent me running. But not this. The heat between us, the mutual respect, and growing love. Yes, love. Somewhere along this wild journey, I'd fallen for the big alien warrior. If he did turn out to be a cocky commander like I'd first thought, well, he was *my* cocky commander. And I planned to claim him right back.

"Are you sure, Jane?" His body shuddered; the weight of his question not lost on me. I held his fate, our future, in my hands with one word. But I had no doubts.

"Yes." I kissed him hard, my hands tangling in his hair. When I pulled back, I added, "Here. Now. We claim each other."

His lips parted. A light radiated behind his eyes. The open adoration on his face undid me. He stared at me like I was the center of the universe. "I am humbled by this gift, ljona." He put our foreheads together, speaking softly. "I will not fail you."

"I know." I broke us apart and chuckled. "But if you don't fuck me now, Tor, I swear to all the stars above, you'll regret it."

His deep barreling laugh tickled my senses. "As you wish, my mate."

An inferno of needed sparked in my core. I had never wanted anyone so much. If I didn't see equal need in his eyes, I'd have been frightened by the intensity of it. But I wasn't alone. With Tor in my life, I would never be alone again.

He laid me down in the blue field, the grass a soft tickling sensation against my back. Unwrapping the fabric from my breasts, he undid the ties as if a priceless treasure rested beyond them.

"Mate," I chided, drawing his gaze to my face. "I don't want slow. I need you now."

He pushed my hands over my head, which arched my breasts up and on display. "You will not rush me, my Truxoria. I have waited too long for you to end this quickly."

"Please," I whined. The need ripping through me too much to handle. "I can't wait." Freeing one of my hands, he reached down my body and thrust two thick fingers in my pussy. I cried out at the delicious sensation. "Yes, more!"

"You are hungry for me." He sucked my breast into his mouth, thrusting his fingers in and out of my core. "I will not keep you wanting then."

His tongue vibrated against my stiff peak as his fingers worked me over. "Tor! Tor!" The pressure built inside me, coiling like a valve that needed release.

He pushed the heel of his hand against my clit, rubbing the tender spot. "Oh fuck. Yes!" My climax ripped through me as I clamped down on his fingers. I screamed his name, the waves of pleasure ebbing and flowing, setting every nerve afire. I was limp as a noodle, and yet, I wanted more.

"I need it now, my mate." I grabbed him around the waist with my legs, pulling him in. "I need you."

"Jane." He took my chin in one hand. "If I take you, you understand what this means?"

I nodded, trying to think through the flames of lust firing within me.

"It's more than a marriage. It's unlike anything you have on Earth." He put his weight on top of me, letting me feel his thick cock and crux—that perfect top-cock— against my pussy. "We will be one. We will speak in each other's minds. Our connection will be unbreakable. Do you want that?"

I cast him a shrewd grin. "I am Jane Kadaran, bossy alien. I know what I want. And when I make up my mind, there's no changing it." I pulled his chest flush against mine. "How many times do I have to tell you? Now, make us one, my cocky commander."

His eyes lit up, and I knew I'd gotten through to him at last. Like me, he'd been through some shit. We'd have more demons to confess no doubt, but we'd do so as a team. The past shaped us, but it would not keep us from becoming who we were meant to be—together.

Then, all thoughts flew from my mind as he notched his cock at the entrance of my pussy. A tight fit had him stealing an inch at a time before he was buried balls deep inside me. We both moaned.

"You feel so good, my Truxoria." His arms were banded steel around me, keeping the majority of his weight on his forearms. "I would stay this way for all time."

"That might be a bit much." I laughed, wrapping my legs around him. "Let's start with now and work our way up to it."

He responded by sliding almost all the way free, then thrusting in hard.

"Fuck! Again," I cried.

"Greedy," he laughed doing it again and again. "Your pussy wants to keep me, it's gripping so hard. Let me help you." Spearing his arms under my back, he lifted up onto his knees with me in tow. The angle meant I couldn't escape his cock.

I threw my head back and moaned.

With me in his lap, my legs still around him, he bounced me on his cock. The impact was so intense, I saw stars. When his crux vibrated against my swollen clit, I screamed again and again. The sensations overwhelmed me. I was lost in a sea of feeling. My orgasm hit like a tsunami, my pussy clamping his cock in a death grip. It triggered his release as he thrust inside me, his cum filling me up. I had no anchor to orient to as I floated in that euphoric state.

Then, I heard his voice in my head. "My Jane, my Truxoria." His words called me to shore and brought me home. "We are One."

13

Tor

IF I COULD STRETCH ONE MOMENT INTO ETERNITY AND live in it for all time, I'd choose this, holding her in my arms forever. I had never experienced such stillness, the universe falling away into nothing. All that remained was her head against my chest and the beating of our connected hearts.

Sated and content, I wished never to let her go. *You fill the parts of me that have been empty for so long.* I spoke in her head, the mating mind-speak possible now that our bond was complete.

I'm home in your embrace. Her voice flowed in my mind, warm and strong like my mate. *You make me feel safe.*

"You are safe with me, Jane." I tilted her chin to meet my gaze and said the words aloud so she might hear the power in them. "You always will be."

She hummed her reply, her eyes growing glassy. "I wish we could stay like this."

"As do I." Her sentiment echoed mine, but we had one more trial to endure before we could finish our mission. Although if they all ended like this, then I'd be eager for the next.

The golden door slid open. I rose to my feet, reaching a hand to help Jane to hers. She readjusted her clothes while I did the same. Calia stood smiling in the doorway. "Another test passed!" she cried. "I am so happy for you both."

"Yes, um." Jane's flushed cheeks and tousled hair hinted at our mating.

I wanted to shout it proudly to the heavens that this glorious Terran female was mine, but I knew she was shyer of such matters. "Thank you, Calia," I filled in smoothly. "We are most grateful for your support."

Jane blinked up at me, her eyelids fluttering. *Thank you for that.*

Her use of our mind-speak set my soul on fire. The easy, carefree manner in which our thoughts flowed to each other was a testament to our bond. I couldn't wait to speak to her in the intimate fashion when my cock was buried inside her. The picturing of it had my lust rising, despite our recent mating.

Tor, Jane's warning tone in my head had me laughing inside. Some of my imaging must have slipped to my mate. Mind-speak didn't mean we could read each other's thoughts. We had to intentionally speak to one another; the same manner in which we would do so aloud. But sometimes if a mate's thoughts were a bit… robust, they'd pass to the other. *Don't you dare laugh. We need to stop thinking with our lower parts and prep for this third test.*

Well, if the last is anything like the first two… I let the thought trail off into the memory of us locked together.

Jane sucked in a breath beside me. "You are impossible."

The plants parted as Calia strode toward us. "The test of truth is a great challenge. Many do not get past it." She beamed with happiness, the emotion evident in her every word and action. The Kinsian's support of our endeavor was a true kindness, rare in this universe. "I am so proud."

"That's so nice of you to say." Jane patted at her hair, trying to tame the wild curls.

Leave them be. I love your hair. I stared pointedly at the hand swatting at her hair.

She rolled her eyes and continued talking to the Kinsian. "Did you say it was a test of truth?"

"Oh yes!" Calia gave that one-handed clap, the common gesture of her species. "The palace determined that your first test would be one of pleasure, and the second one of truth."

"Of pleasure and truth?" Jane's forehead wrinkled.

"Indeed, the first was to see your physical compatibility, and the second was to test your mental connection."

It had a certain logic to it, but the trials appeared to be more about testing the bond between us than the material we sought. I asked as much aloud. "Why would it choose to test us on such things when we're here to seek the ergamite for our people?"

Calia bade us follow her through the doorway. The sight of the infinite hall was growing old, and I yearned more than ever to complete this assignment. I'd broken my vow not to claim my mate before ensuring the mission's success. Yet, I could not be angry for it, not with our souls bound as one, and emotions flowing through me as easily as water in a stream.

"Sometimes," Calia spun to face us, taking our hands in each one of hers and then bringing them together, "we don't know what we seek, even when it is in front of us."

Jane smiled up at me, squeezing my hand, and then turned to Calia. "Those are wise words."

"I agree." I held her hand to my chest, then let it go. "But what of the ergamite? We cannot leave without it."

"Fear not." The Kinsian whirled around and continued down the hall, passing multiple doors as she led us onward. "Your third test is the final step. Prove your bond, and all that you seek shall be revealed."

"Can you tell us what the third test is?" Jane asked as we followed.

"I'm afraid I cannot reveal that, until you've completed it. I'm sorry." Calia stopped at a plain brown door. It had grooves in the wood grain and a charcoal handle. Glancing at us, she hesitated before opening the door.

"Calia?" Jane placed a gentle, steadying hand on the Kinsian's shoulder. "Are you all right?"

She seemed to snap back to herself at my mate's touch and blinked her large round eyes. "Yes, it's just…" Pushing the door on its hinges, it swung open to reveal a stone passageway. "Be careful."

I nodded to our attendant. Truly, thankful for her and her mate's help. "We will."

"Good." Her smile was small but genuine. "Lorn and I shall meet you when you've completed your task."

Jane whispered a final "thank you" to Calia as we stepped into the tunnel. The door closed with a creak behind us. "So, this is different."

I ducked my head to avoid injury as the passage rose to my height or lower in several spots. "It is at that, my mate."

We walked side-by-side with little space between us. The tunnel continued to narrow, until we had to shift to a single line. Jane led the way, and I watched our backs. But soon a light flickered not far from us, revealing the end of this stone nightmare. By the time we reached it, I had hunched over almost in half.

"Phew," Jane straightened and stretched as we emerged. "That was not fun."

I hummed my agreement as I scanned our new environment. The scenery was…odd. It gave the appearance of open space, as if we were in a jungle on some unknown planet. Yet, this had to be a room like the others. A scarlet mountain range indicated a distant border, but the remainder gave no hint that we were inside the palace. Thin trees with trunks no wider than my wrist reached toward an endless cloud-filled sky. Hot, humid hair caused our clothes to stick to our skin.

"This is something," Jane commented as she touched her palm to the ground. Brown soil fell from her hand as she scooped it up and let it go. "Reminds me of dirt from Earth."

I searched the horizon for signs of a curved wall, but all I saw was empty sky. "I can't see anything that indicates the end of the room. Do you?"

"No." Jane rose, shielding her eyes from a bright orange sun streaming from above. "Do you think the passage led us outside?"

I pictured the landing platform where we arrived and the surrounding region of golden sand. "I don't believe so. It doesn't match the terrain we saw earlier."

"A holo-projection then? Like the one on your ship."

"It's possible." The space fighter's holo-room could project an outdoor environment with fair accuracy, but not an infinite space. If this were a holo-projection, it would be the largest and most sophisticated I'd ever seen.

"Well, whatever it is," Jane swatted at an insect flying in front of her face, "we need to figure out what we're supposed to do here and finish this."

I waggled my brows. "I have ideas."

She slapped my arm. *The faster we get the ergamite, the quicker we can get back to the ship.* Her mouth twisted into an evil grin. *And it is a long trip home. How will we occupy the time?*

I wanted to show her exactly how I planned to fill the time—and her. But a crash through the trees caught my eye. The trunks curved to the sides, parting a path. Through the split in the jungle trees, a creature emerged. It had to be ten times my size. Its orange fur shone as if absorbing the sunlight and matching its hue. A wide, gaping maw held a single fang in its center. It walked on two thick hind legs and pushed the trees aside with its four arms. When a branch snapped in its face, it threw its head back and roared. Its powerful arms beat its chest in a fit of fury.

"Holy shit!" Jane cried, her eyes widening with the sight of the creature. "It's like a cross between a gorilla and a saber tooth tiger, except it's huge."

I didn't know what either of those creatures were, but this beast was unlike any I'd known. And we had no weapons. "Jane," I said softly, not wanting to startle her and chance drawing the beast's attention. "Stay behind me and move toward the passage."

"What?" Her gaze shifted to me. "We can't run. What if the test is to face this thing?"

"Truxoria." I grabbed her arm and pulled her close to me. "We carry no weapons. And I will not lose you in a fruitless battle."

Her eyes narrowed. "What are you planning, Tor?"

Drav it. I cursed, shielding my thoughts from her. It scratched my insides, feeling unnatural to block her out. But she'd never agree to my plan, and I had only one chance to bring it to fruition. "We have to go back through the tunnel."

"I don't believe you." She crossed her arms over her chest. "I told you, we can't back down."

"Jane, be reasonable." I motioned toward the creature.

"No, you listen here." She poked a finger into my side. "If you think I'm going to hide in that tunnel while you go and fight that giant gorilla-tiger alone, you are out of your damn mind. That clear?"

A smile tugged at my lips, despite our dire situation. My mate knew me too well, guessing my plan before I had a chance to even execute a first step. "I won't lose you, my mate."

"Yeah, and I'm not losing you." Her hands balled into fist. "So, let's not die today."

Fire rose within me, the memory of my mother fading before my eyes as fresh as the day it happened. Her face shifted to Jane's, and I snapped. Grabbing her shoulders, I shook her. "You will not sacrifice yourself."

Her face softened as she stared at me. There was no reproach in her gaze, only a deep empathy. "Tor," she took my hands from her shoulders and held them tight between her breasts, "hear what I'm saying. No one is dying today." Glancing beyond us to the beast in the jungle, she sighed. The creature was pulling trees by the roots and flinging them toward the distant red mountains. "This isn't about sacrifice. Not you for me, or me for you. If you try to fight that beast alone, you will lose." She gave my hands a gentle squeeze. "We are stronger together, and I won't let you stand alone."

I swallowed a lump in my throat. The fear of losing another person I loved was an emotion she understood. Yet, she didn't allow it to stop her from her duty—our duty. "You're right, my Truxoria. We win together," I assessed our odds as I turned my focus on the creature, "or not at all."

"Hey! Don't count us out yet." She released my hands and shrugged. "That thing could be a vegetarian."

I snorted. "You think it's a plant-eater?"

The beast roared to the skies.

"Sure." Her laughter held no mirth. "There's always a chance."

The creature, as if sensing our talk, spotted us at last. Four tiny oval eyes fixed on our position. Its mouth snapped shut, the fang hanging over its chin. It stalked forward. It moved with lithe grace for a beast its size, eating up the ground with long strides. The look in its quadruple gaze was not that of a plant-eater. This was a predator, and it had determined we would be its prey.

"Not today, my orange friend," I muttered. The ground lacked anything we could use as weapons. Vegetative life abounded, but no rocks or anything sharp. Weighing our options, I spoke to Jane. *When I say, run for the tunnel.*

No. We already went through this. I'm staying with you. A whooshing exhale passed her lips. *We'll find a way.*

I already have. Spring to the passage when I give you the word. I gauged the distance of the nearest tree. *He'll follow you. To reach you, he'll have to crouch and use one of his arms to pull you from the tunnel.* My hearts raced as I imagined the beast pawing after her. *Do not let him get you. I'll use the tree like a club and find his weak point.*

As the creature drew closer, its stench filled my nose. It smelled like butra dip, the sweet treat that my brather Brok favored. Except when it rotted it put out an aroma that could gag a warrior. This beast had a matching scent.

"Ugh," Jane cried, covering her mouth. "That's awful."

I resisted the urge to stuff my nose with dirt to block the smell. "Almost time. Be ready."

The soft tissue of its eyes is weak. Her body leaned forward, weight shifting to the balls of her feet. *The skin at its throat, where the fur thins, is possible too.*

My clever mate. I smiled inwardly. The universe had blessed me with a fighter. I had to use her knowledge and skills to win this battle. She was right. If I let my fear rule me, we would lose.

The beast came within striking distance. I shouted to her, "Now!"

Jane shot for the passage while I dove for the tree. Yanking it from the roots, I folded the thin trunk in half, and then in half again. It thickened the wood, creating a flexible but strong makeshift club. I didn't hesitate as the beast flopped onto its stomach and used its furry arm to swipe inside the tunnel after my mate. Striking the two right eyes with my weapon, the beast pulled back its arm and roared. The eyes I struck squeezed shut, but the remaining two whirled to me. I swung again at its throat.

A gurgling howl rent the air. The beast used all four arms to strike, everyone aimed at pummeling me into the ground.

"No," Jane cried as she emerged from the tunnel and ran for me.

I dove for her, twisting onto my back as I landed to take the impact. The creature struck the dirt where I had stood. *I told you to run for the passage.*

You did, and I did. She huffed. *We didn't agree I'd stay there.*

Before we had time to argue further, the beast turned its large body. Its uninjured eyes zeroed in on us. As we scrambled to our feet, a haunting tune permeated the air. The deep melody mixed with a high-pitched harmony, creating a unified composition.

"What is that?" Jane swayed with the music.

The creature froze in mid-step. Its powerful hind leg sank to the ground. Orange eyelids hung heavy. When it dropped to its knees, it tipped over like a tree falling after being chopped down. The crash of its big body flattened all the nearby vegetation.

From the rocky tunnel, Calia and Lorn appeared. Their arms were raised to the sky as their bow-shaped mouths emitted the song. When the beast showed no sign of rising, the music ended. The Kinsian couple strode to where Jane and I stood.

"You have passed the third test," Calia's soft voice was packed with emotion.

Lorn gave his one-handed clap. "Congratulations."

14

Jane

I was too dumbfounded to speak. One moment we were facing off with an orange gorilla-tiger, and the next the beast was lulled to sleep like a baby. "How? Why?"

I hadn't meant to ask the questions aloud, but my mouth ran away from me. The adrenaline from the fight flowed through me, and the confusion of its aftermath meant I had little filter left.

"We didn't defeat the creature." Tor spoke the thought that echoed in my mind.

Calia gave us a kind smile. "Your trial was never to beat the kongana." Her gaze traveled to the animal, a reverent expression on her face. "The test is to determine your willingness to sacrifice for each other." She plucked two flowers from the ground near her feet. "The test of sacrifice is passed."

"You are each willing to give your lives for the other," Lorn continued the explanation. "But the fates, and we," he inclined his head toward his mate, "are impressed by your resolve to stand together."

"The strength of your love, of your bond is clear." Calia presented each of us with one of the golden flowers, tucking them into the fabric across our chests. "You are worthy of what you seek."

"The tests are complete," Lorn shouted and threw his arms toward the sky. "Bring forth the chamber of claiming."

The ground shifted beneath our feet. I stumbled into Tor. He righted me against his side and tucked me in close. His strong, hard body was an anchor for my wayward mind. I held his waist, squeezing the chiseled abs beneath my fingers.

As we watched, the environment transformed from a steamy jungle to a crystal oasis. The orange creature disappeared along with the tall, thin trees and thick vegetation. The walls, which we failed to see before, appeared in a perfect circle, lined with shining gemstones embedded in black marble. A spongy carpet laid beneath our feet. At the center of the room ran a turquoise waterfall into a bean shaped pool. The top of the falls had no source. It simply flowed from a bright white light that filled the ceiling. It likewise had no exit, running continuously into the pool below without overflowing it.

"It's incredible." I breathed in, gasping at the shocking beauty of the place.

"This is the final stop in your journey, my friends." Lorn waved around the room. "Welcome to the chamber of claiming."

"Use the flowers on the altar at the bottom of the falls. Then, demonstrate your bond to the fates." Calia took her mate's hand. "When you tap into the depths of your desires, what you seek will become yours."

"More hints?" Tor crossed his arms over his chest, but his words held no heat. "It seems you've given us snippets of advice before every test."

Calia laughed, her voice like raindrops. "Why, Commander, we would never interfere with the tests of seeking."

"Of course not." He dropped his arms and grinned at the Kinsians.

"When you have claimed what you need, the falls will shift into a form appropriate for travel and return you to your ship." Lorn stepped forward and held out his hand. "We will not see you again."

Tor gripped the Kinsian male's forearm, a warrior's honor. "Then, we will not be able to show our gratitude."

"Your success is all the thanks we need." Calia turned to me and wrapped her arms around my shoulders. "Be well."

Tears stung my eyes. I had never known such selfless people. "Thank you for everything."

"Do not be sad, my friend Jane." She pulled from the embrace, smiling as she did. "The universe is a magical place. You never know when we may meet again."

I laughed. "You know someone else said almost the exact thing to me."

A twinkle sparked in her bulbous eyes. "Then, you can trust it is true."

"I think you're right." I hugged her one final time and turned to shake Lorn's hand. Tor gave Calia a warrior's grip to her slender forearm too, gentle with his hold.

As the pair turned to leave through a door of glistening silver, a deep sense of knowing gathered inside me. As if the universe itself spoke through me I said, "May the stars guide you, and their light shine within you."

Calia gifted me a final smile over her shoulder before leaving with her mate.

"They saved us, you know." I turned to Tor, holding a sniffle at bay.

He held me close, his warmth against my skin. "They did."

We stayed that way for a while, just holding each other and taking in all that had happened. Eventually, the sound of the waterfall and the call to finish our mission spurred us on.

Tor brought forth his flower. "What do you think we do with these?"

"Well," I reclaimed my flower from inside the fabric and held it up to my nose, "Calia said there's an altar at the bottom of the waterfall. Let's see what happens when we put them on it."

When we reached the edge of the pool, I slipped off my sandals and toed the water. "It's warm."

Tor didn't hesitate to strip off his clothes. My jaw dropped as he stood in all his naked glory, only the tiny flower fisted in his large hand. His cock was hard and standing at attention. The crux atop it equally ready for action. "If you keep looking at me like that, I'll claim you again."

I blinked. "Maybe that's exactly what we're supposed to do."

He strode toward me, eyes burning with need. "What do you mean, my mate?"

Calia said we had to demonstrate our bond to the fates and tap into the depths of our desires, I said in our mind-speak. I pulled the crisscrossed fabric over my head, peeling it to my waist. Then, I pushed it over my hips and down my legs. When I stood naked before him, I resisted the urge to cover myself. I was not ashamed of my body, but I couldn't say I was too comfortable hanging out in my birthday suit either.

That is a feeling we will soon remedy, little captain.

"Caught that thought, did you?" I frowned at him.

Only because you thought it so loud. He chuckled in my mind as he guided me to the water. "If I could keep you naked all the time, I would have it so."

I rolled my eyes, but it was an exasperated affection for my cocky commander. Following him into the pool, I felt the bottom slope as it gradually declined. I took his flower from him and held his and mine above the waterline to be safe. I didn't know what would happen if they got wet. *Though I suppose it will when we place it on the altar.*

"Let's find out." Tor bade me come to him. "Wrap your legs around me. You're tall, but I believe it will go over your head as we get closer."

He was right. As we waded through the pool, it deepened in the middle toward the base of the falls. Only Tor's head and the tops of his shoulders remained above the water. He kept me above it with a firm grip on my ass. I held the flowers safe.

"There it is." I motioned toward a slab hidden by the curtain of water from the falls. I caught a glimpse of it as the water separated for a second. The altar was no bigger than my arm, but it rested just behind where the falls met the pool.

"We'll have to go through it."

I cupped the flowers to my chest, protecting them as best as I could with my hands. "Do it."

Tor cut powerful strides through the water. I held my breath as we ducked under the falls. The shock of water was surprisingly refreshing, even as it soaked my hair. I shook the drops from my eyes and checked on the flowers. Their golden petals glistened with droplets, but they didn't wilt. "They seem okay."

"Good, put them there." Carrying me to the altar, Tor hoisted me higher.

The slab was an unadorned piece of stone. It sat behind the falls, safe from its splashes and dry as a bone on top. I placed both flowers in the middle, then dropped into the water with Tor. Waiting with held breath, we stared at the flowers.

Nothing happened.

As Tor held me in his embrace, my legs around his waist and my arms about his neck, I knew my earlier assessment was right. My body heated, even in the comfortable warmth of the water. "Whatever is meant to happen with those flowers," I palmed his cheek, looking into his captivating eyes, "it won't until we prove our bond."

"Then, let us give the fates a show, little captain." He glided toward a shallow part of the pool behind the falls.

My heart picked up the rhythm of the rushing water, my desire for him growing with every beat. "You know, I think I'm starting to like when you call me that, cocky commander."

He barked a laugh. "That's good," he fisted my hair and pulled my head back, "because I don't intend to stop." His teeth scraped my neck along the tender spot where it met my shoulder. He bit down just enough for me to squirm in his hold. He squeezed my ass. *Don't move, my ljona.* Licking the spot where he bit, he worked a path to my ear. *Your skin is meant to bear my marks.*

My legs tightened around his waist. *Then, mark me.*

He doubled his efforts at my words, nipping and licking my neck, then my collarbone and at last my breasts. I thrust them up into his seeking mouth, the water splashing around us. When he sucked on the side, leaving his mark, I moaned. *More.* He did it again, and again, leaving love bites in his wake. My nipples were hard and aching, but he did not leave me wanting. Laving them with attention, he used that amazing tongue of his to vibrate against the tips.

"Oh yes!" My hips began a seeking rhythm beneath the water.

"I must have you, my mate. Are you ready?" He moved me to a shallow bed where my shoulders rested against the incline of the pool while my hips and ass remained underwater.

Yes, so ready. I moaned, needing him inside me.

I've pictured taking you while speaking in your mind. He knelt in the water. His cock-head angled to my pussy. *I want to feel you clench those tight pussy walls around me.* He thrust inside slowly, opening me to his invasion. *You take me so well, Jane.*

Tor. Even my inner voice was hot and needy. But his words in my head amped up my desire. I didn't think I could want him more, but my body said otherwise. *Fuck me, please.* I was beyond caring about begging. I wanted everything he could give me and more.

With pleasure. Guiding my ankles to his shoulders and grabbing a firm hold on my hips, he pulled out and thrust in hard. That delicious crux slid along my clit as he did so.

Again! I cried.

He did, his thrusts rocking the water around us. As the pace increased and with nothing to hold onto, I palmed my breasts. *Yes, my mate, hold them for me. Pinch those sweet tits.*

I did as he said, rolling my nipples between my fingers. The action sent zings of pleasure straight to my clit. The slide of his crux coupled with those sensations brought me to the precipice. Then, his crux vibrated. *Fuck! I'm going to come.*

Yes, Jane. Come for me. And scream my name.

"Tor!" His cock hit that sensitive spot inside me as his crux took care of my clit. I came so hard the water splashed around me and the sound of the waterfall rushed in my ears. I floated, suspended by the water or the intensity of my climax, I didn't know. Or care.

His orgasm hit soon after, the thick cum filling me. Still hard inside me, I squeezed his cock. It sent aftershocks zipping through me. So, I did it again.

Keep that up and I'll claim you again. He guided my legs back to the water, but he didn't pull out of me.

I squeezed him more. *I might want you to.*

A spark gleamed in his eyes. Grabbing my knee, he turned me on my side. The sensation of his cock inside me with the half-spin felt so good. Straddling my bottom leg, he placed it so it rested between his. Then, he took my top leg and brought my calf to his shoulder. The side position opened me in a new way that was hot as fuck.

Again, Jane? He began a slow, torturous grind into my pussy. His cock hitting me in new spots as he circled his hips.

Yes, yes! Don't stop. I dug my nails into the pool's floor.

He chuckled. *I didn't plan to.* The ride was a steady, even pace that drove me out of my mind. Whenever I got close to the edge, he stopped, holding his cock inside me.

Tor. I didn't know if I was whining or warning him, but the more he worked me up and paused, the more intense the sensations built. *I can't keep this up.*

You don't have to. I can for both of us.

His movements were measured and controlled, designed to make me wild. But I wanted to make him just as out of his head with wanting. Every time he stopped, I squeezed him harder. My pussy walls fluttered around him. Then, I reached down between us and palmed his crux.

Jane, he warned.

But I was done with his teasing. I ran my nails against his crux, loving the feel of the hard top cock in my hand. *Crex that feels good.* His thrusts increased, and I matched his pace as I stroked his crux.

No more stopping. I held him immobile in my hand for a second. *You stop, I stop.*

Wicked female. He laughed in my mind. But he didn't stop again.

The smooth glide of his cock in and out, the strokes to his crux, culminated in a second climax that hit us at the same time. I screamed and held his crux as he pumped his cum into me again. It overflowed my pussy, seeping down my thighs. My inner walls clenched tight.

I sighed.

"Is that the sound of a well-pleased mate?" He let my leg rest by my side and slowly pulled from my pussy. Although sated, I mourned the loss.

"Yes, it is." I closed my eyes and waved at him with a flopping arm. "Now, I need to sleep for a year."

I felt his smile in my mind. "In the water?"

"Anywhere." I yawned.

Picking me up like I was a precious treasure, he held me in his lap in the pool's shallow depths. "Do you not want our reward?"

I perked up at that, lifting my head from his shoulder. "Reward?"

"Look over there." He pointed to the altar under the falls where the two golden flowers glowed. Before our eyes they transformed into two rich gemstones as big as my head.

I gasped, recalling the report I'd read before our mission. "Ergamite."

"It is." Tor's voice held a note of awe. "It's the biggest deposit I've ever seen. A sliver of it could power a shield around Earth for half of your solar year. This size…"

"It'll keep it running forever." I slid from his hold. "What are we waiting for? Let's get it!"

His answering laughter warmed my soul. "I don't think it's going anywhere, Jane."

"Well, we are." I wrapped my arms around him and placed a kiss on his nose. "It's time to go home."

15

Tor

HOME. IT HAD BEEN LONGER THAN I COULD COUNT SINCE I'd seen my planet. After my maether's death, and then later my paether's, I hadn't felt like I had a home anymore. But now? *Jane.* She was it. Wherever we went, no matter what the fates had in mind, if I was with her, I'd always be home.

Gathering the ergamite, we waded through the water and to the side of the pool in which we'd entered. On the shore, our original clothes waited for us, including my vest full of daggers, and a basket of food. The note atop the basket was written in a delicate handwriting. It read in universal standard, "In case you get hungry." It was signed with a C and an L.

"They truly are the most wonderful people." Jane hugged the card to her breast.

"I can't disagree." I put the ergamite next to the basket and reached for our clothes. I slid my pants over my hips and my arms through my vest. I tapped the daggers beneath, feeling more at ease with their weight against my chest. My boots were most welcome after the thin sandals. "Are you ready to leave?"

Jane dressed in her pants, sleeveless shirt, and boots. A hair tie from her pocket pinned her hair atop her head in that circular style she liked. While I loved when her hair brushed against my skin, I wanted her to be her most comfortable and authentic self. She was beautiful, regardless of her hairstyle or clothes.

With a last look around, she turned those incredible blue eyes to me. "Yes," she said with a wistful smile. "A part of me is going to miss this place. So much happened here." Sliding her fingers through mine, she brought our joined hands between her breasts. "But I'm ready."

As if sensing our needs, the water rose and transformed in the air. The molecules bunched together to form a solid, circular pod. The waterfall disappeared along with the pool, leaving behind a smooth surface. The pod landed on it, and a ramp extended from its center.

"Yeah, that's still cool." Jane waved at our new ride. *Think its tech or magic?*

I'm not sure I believe in magic. I picked up the basket and the ergamite.

She scoffed. *No magic? The Rhonar have literal fated mates. Like one person in all the universe to complete you. And even after all your people have lost, you somehow, against all odds, have begun to find them again.* Her arms wrapped around my waist, tickling my ribs. With my arms full, I couldn't stop her. *No magic. What a silly thing to say, my cocky commander.* She let me go, lifting the second ergamite and heading for the ramp.

My mate *did* have a point.

I followed her inside. The interior was a simple design. A flat, circular bench lined the perimeter with ample seating. A center console projected a holographic map. The controls had their purpose spelled out in universal standard. I placed our supplies in a storage box under the bench and headed for the console.

"Well, this is simple enough." Jane swiped through the holographic projection.

I set the controls to rendezvous with our ship. "For now," I reminded my mate. "But we still need to get the ergamite back to Earth."

"Don't be negative," she chided, reviewing the coordinates. "We've got this far."

The ceiling opened to reveal the planet's orange sky, and the pod lifted off. Using the highest point of the Prism Palace like a slingshot, it launched us in a circle toward the landing bay. The refracted light of the sun against the prismatic towers cast rainbow hues on all it touched.

The pod connected with our ship, and within moments, we were standing in our own vessel.

"Ah." Jane sighed as we filed in and headed for the bridge. "It's good to be back." I packed the ergamite safely away and took the pilot's chair. Jane was already navigating our course home. "How do you want to play this, Commander?" She shot me a grin, then her expression turned serious. "We can't use stealth mode the whole ride, can we?"

"Unfortunately, no." I checked our reserves, determining how and when to best engage the shielding. "It'll deplete our energy and strand us in space."

"Hmm," she tapped her nail against her chin, "that's a technical flaw we'll have to figure out and fix when we get back home."

"Are you planning a new career in engineering?" I chuckled, setting the ship for launch.

She snorted. "Hardly. It's the Captain's life for me. But I do have a tech genius aboard the moonbase," she paused, and her eyes twinkled with mirth, "even if she does have the worst taste in clothing."

I pictured Jane in the sexy outfits I'd spotted in her bags. "If she's responsible for your packed garments, then I'd have to disagree."

Swatting my arm, she smirked. "I might be persuaded to wear one or two." A shudder ran through her. "But *not* in public again."

"Fair enough." I was more than happy to keep my Jane all to myself.

The space fighter took off, and I engaged stealth shielding. We shot through the planet's atmosphere and into space. The Mangox knew our destination as Sense VII, so between here and their outpost would be the most dangerous part of the trip. We had to get free of their territory and to the coordinates where we could employ the wormhole generator and return to Earth's solar system. But the Meta Sector was vast, and the Mangox had spies everywhere. If we tried to use stealth mode from here to the coordinates, we wouldn't make it.

I wrestled with the problem as the computer monitored the space around us. It was quiet. Uncomfortably quiet.

The tension pinged back and forth. I could feel Jane working through our dilemma too. I caught snippets of her thoughts as she subconsciously projected them to me. Then, she snapped her fingers. "Are there other Rhonar in the sector?"

My brows winged up. "There are." My fingers flew over the controls. "They're in search of the lost science team from your missing deep space vessel." It was a testament to my mate's leadership skills that she would think to call for aid. "Computer, put out a message on the encoded channel to all Rhonar vessels in the area. We are in need of an escort."

Spans later, we passed the Mangox outpost. Yet, we hadn't received an answer to our hail. My mind continued to work over the problem, and I could think of only one solution, one method to get a message to my brathers that would not fail.

"I'm going to call a florin." I turned to Jane, watching her response. "Did your sister tell you about them?"

"The fluffy empathetic creatures who help the Rhonar with their lack of emotions?" Her mouth crinkled, affection clear on her face. "Oh yeah, Sage would not shut up about them. Said they're the cutest beings in the universe, tied with the space otter-creatures she met when her and Brok crash landed on that planet."

"The gyorpins," I supplied, remembering fondly the aliens who had helped my brather and his mate.

"Yes, those guys. But anyway, how can you call a florin?" Her head cocked to the side. "And how will that help us?"

"The florin are inter-dimensional beings. If they're in a parallel space to ours, then they can hear our call. And if our message reached my brathers, the florin could guide them to us." I shrugged. "If it didn't, they should be able to relay it to them."

Her eyes widened. "Then, why not call one before?"

I scrubbed a hand over the back of my neck. "We'll have to disengage stealth shields."

Silence fell between us. She scanned the Meta Sector star charts. "Is there anywhere we can get what we need to keep the shields running?"

I shook my head. "Even if we could find an outpost or planet to energize the ship, we'd still have to turn off the shielding to do it."

"What about the ergamite?" She eyed the storage unit where it laid.

"It may be possible. I don't know for certain, but not without modifications to the ship." I tightened my fists. "Same problem either way."

Her mouth twisted into a grimace. "Then, there's no choice. We have to risk it."

"I concur." Pulling up the navigational controls, I scanned the sector. "Computer, are any ships detected in two parsecs of our location?"

"Negative," the computer intoned. "No ships detected."

"What if there are ships in stealth mode?" Jane spun her chair toward me. "Would the computer detect them?"

My jaw clenched. "No."

She inhaled slowly, and then blew it out on a long exhale. "Okay, then."

I reached for her and took her hands in mine. "Computer, scan for any energy signatures, same radius."

"Scanning." The beats ticked on. Jane and I stared into each other's eyes. "No energy signatures identified."

I leaned in and claimed her lips, a slow kiss filled with longing. I poured everything I felt into that kiss, all that I hoped for our future. When I pulled back at last, her gaze held mine captive. Her eyes were glassy, but her voice was solid as she said, "Do it."

I kept my gaze locked on those ocean blue eyes as I commanded the computer. "Disengage stealth mode."

A crackle of energy sounded, and the shields went down. "Florin!" I shouted the instant they did. It took several beats, but a florin appeared. "You?"

The emerald florin who had helped me not long ago, bounced around the control console. He sent me a plethora of images, all documenting the journey Jane and I had taken since leaving the moonbase.

"You've been keeping tabs on us then?" I raised a brow at him.

The little empath had the sense to look chagrined.

"Oh stars!" Jane cried and hopped up from her seat. "Sage wasn't lying. He's the cutest creature I've ever seen."

The florin held its paw to her, a giant smile pushing out its puffy cheeks.

"Aww, he's sending me, like, happy feelings." She squinted as if she could see through the florin. "It's hard to explain. I feel them, but I know he's doing it."

"Yes, that's a fair description." I waved at the florin to regain his focus. "My friend, I've sent a message to my brathers in the sector. We need their help to make it safely back to Earth."

The florin tucked his three tails under him and used them like a chair to sit. He sent me feelings of understanding.

"I need you to find them and guide them to us." I knelt to stare in his dark, round eyes and ensure he comprehended our situation. "If they haven't received our message, then you need to explain things as best you can. Whatever you do, get them here."

Leaping off the console with his tail as the spring, he landed on the floor and nodded his head vigorously. He sent an image of him with other Rhonar and projected feelings of calm. Then, he popped from our dimension.

"Whoa," Jane whispered. "That was…um…easy?"

I sighed as a warning symbol appeared on the screen. "It's about to get harder. The stealth shielding has used too much energy. We won't be able to re-engage it."

Reclaiming our seats, we didn't speak as the ship continued onward. It was another span later, when she said, *I'm afraid to break the silence. Like it would be a jinx or something.*

I know, Ijona. I feel the same. I cocked my head toward her. *There are other ways to distract ourselves.*

She laughed as I intended. *That sounds so much more appealing than staring into space—literally.* Her hands came to rest atop the console, fingertips pressing together. *But you know neither of us are leaving the bridge.*

I did. My Truxoria and I had differences that balanced each other, but in many aspects, we were the same. Our devotion to our people, our dedication to duty, and most of all, our need for control, all culminated together to guarantee that neither of us was going anywhere. We'd sleep in our piloting chairs, if we had to, but it was more likely we would not rest, until we got the ergamite to Earth.

When the alarms went off around the ship, rest was the last thing we had to worry about. "Report."

"Incoming Mangox vessel approaching at bearing 201 mark 11."

"Shit!" Jane programmed the screen to the coordinates. An image of a battle cruiser took up the entire space. "What are the odds it's the same ship?"

An incoming transmission roared through our speakers. "Rhonar vessel, cease your engines in the name of Capo Mulo."

I ground my back teeth. "Draving good, I'd say."

Her hands flew over the controls. "Evasive maneuvers."

"Acknowledged." I yanked on the steering column and put the ship in manual flight. If we had any chance of escaping, I needed to throw off their targeting. "Use the controls by your right hand and keep the hyperdrive active."

"Roger that," she said with deadly calm.

"Weapons system online." Banking to the left, I narrowly avoided a strike from their projectile.

A series of clicks, and the computer said, "Weapons ready."

"Jane, column to your left, use our lasers to fire back at these bastards."

I caught her icy smile from the corner of my eye. "Happily."

Space ignited with back-and-forth volleys. A graze to our starboard side, knocked out our auto-targeting. I re-engaged the system and gave Jane manual control.

"Damn bastards," she spat as she aimed the laser shots at the underside of their hull.

We had the advantage of being smaller and lighter, able to maneuver easily around their bulk. But if they landed a direct hit on us, we'd be goners.

A wailing alarm stopped my hearts. "Fire in engineering block one." The computer's even voice pierced my nerves. "Beginning auto-extinguish sequence."

"We can't keep this up, Tor." Her knuckles turned white around the weapons' controls.

I know, ljona. My kedara surged through my veins. I had not spent a lifetime seeking my mate to lose her now. I sent a silent prayer to the stars. *Celestia, help us. See us through.*

"Anti-projectile system failing," the computer announced. "Targeting breached. Impact imminent."

A cacophonous boom pierced the chaotic battle. Fires ignited across the hull of the Mangox battle cruiser. The flames spread, until it was nothing but a hulking pile of metal in space.

Jane released her death grip on the controls. "What the——?

"Greetings, brather!" A Rhonar warrior's voice came over the speakers.

I sucked in a breath. "Computer, on screen."

A male with long black hair and two swords strapped to his back appeared. "Commander Torian." He put his fist to his sternum and bowed his head."It has been too long."

I rose from my chair and mirrored his movements. "Raiker, my old friend, fair meet."

Another Rhonar shouldered the first, a set of three spearheads peaking from over his shoulder. "Perhaps, not so fair, Tor, if we find you in this mess."

"Firas," I snorted and sucked my tongue at his antics.

Raiker shoved the other male out of view. "I told you to knock it off, you draving fool."

"Come on, I'm only playing." Firas' voice floated to us from off screen.

"Enough." Raiker sighed. "Sorry, Commander. We've had our hands full up here."

"Can't wait to hear all about it." I motioned toward my little captain who had a smile on her face. "But first, meet my Truxoria, Jane Kadaran." I tugged her out of the chair and to my side. "And Raiker?"

"Yes, Commander?"

I kissed my mate soundly, my hearts beating only for her, before I turned my attention back to my Rhonar brather. "Get us the crex home."

Epilogue

JANE

"Whoa!" Sage flipped the popcorn bucket, sending kernels in every direction.

Taylor tugged it from her grip, whining, "No more for you. You've lost more than half to the floor."

The two sat on my navy-colored couch in my quarters, freaking out over every detail of my journey. "You know you're both cleaning this up."

"Yeah, yeah." Sage waved at me as if the popcorn decorating my rug was of no consequence. "We'll do it. Now, keep going."

"Speak for yourself," Taylor muttered, guarding the bucket like it was a ring of power.

"That's everything. The Rhonar saved us from the Mangox attack and guided us back to the coordinates." I downplayed the severity of the attack and how close we'd come to not making it home. No need to scare them. "Then, we used the wormhole generator and came home." I snagged some popcorn as Taylor narrowed her eyes at me. "You two have to make some serious tweaks to that by the way, ladies. That is not a fun ride."

"Yeah, tell me about it." Sage snorted.

Taylor rolled her eyes. "It's not like we can control a trip through a wormhole. We're basically using it to punch temporary holes in space." She plopped more of the buttery treat into her mouth. "Be thankful it works at all."

"Fair, fair." I leaned on the arm of the couch and stretched my legs. "I have another job for you anyway, Taylor."

She perked up at that. "Oh yeah?"

"Wait!" Sage held up her hand. "What happened to the other Rhonar first? You said they found one of the lost crew members from DS1?"

"Right." I snapped my fingers. "I forgot that part." Snagging my holo-pad, I pulled up the details on the lost vessel. "So, this is the roster of the missing." I scrolled through the list. "Ava was the first found, which you know led the Rhonar to earth. But other teams of their warriors are traveling the different sectors in search of the abducted crew and science team."

"Didn't the scientists make it off the ship as the attack took place?" Sage's gaze scanned over the list.

"Yes." I stopped on a picture of a security officer, Elena Rivera. "The crew helped evacuate most of the science team before they were abducted. But now, one of the personnel has been found. This woman."

Taylor jumped up, spilling more popcorn.

Sage gave her a side eye. "You are so cleaning this with me."

She waved off my sister's remarks. "That's incredible. This means we have more leads, right?"

"Sort of. Elena was rescued from a *pleasure cruiser*." I made the sign for quotation marks in the air. "At least that's what the bastards who kidnapped her claimed it to be."

"Guess it wasn't, huh?" Sage snagged the bucket back.

"No. It was a cover for a slave market." I put down the holo-pad and rose from the couch. "But no other humans were aboard. So, the Rhonar are back to square one in the search."

The bottom of my couch took a wallop as Sage kicked it. "Damn."

"Yeah, my thoughts too." I whirled toward the blond tech genius. "But that's where Taylor comes in?"

Her hazel eyes widened, and she squeaked, "Me?"

"Yes, you." I smiled and strode to my side table. Grabbing the flash key, I handed it to Taylor. "You're going to figure out how to make stealth shielding last on the Rhonar space fighters—and ours when we start building them—without draining the energy supplies."

Her tongue peeked out from the side of her mouth as her eyes narrowed in thought.

Sage smiled at our friend, and then looked at me. "And what about you, Captain?" A knowing look passed her face. "What are you going to do?"

I crouched beside my sister and snagged an arm around her shoulders. "I, my nosy sister, am going to spend time with my new mate." I tweaked her nose. "And then, I'm going to make sure our government officials stick to their end of the deal."

"And perhaps, a double wedding?" Her brows wiggled. "You wouldn't have to be a bridesmaid then."

I laughed. "You are sneaky."

Taylor paid us no mind, already using her holo-pad to read over the information the Rhonar provided on their stealth technology. "You know, Miach, would probably be helpful with this." She swiped through the information faster than I could have read it. "I know he's their healer, but he's brilliant. And he's been helping us make their medical tech compatible with ours."

"And he's also gorgeous, funny, and a doctor," Sage teased.

Taylor grabbed the popcorn bucket and dumped it over my sister's head.

I howled with laughter. "Okay, I'm going to see my hot alien, and you two are cleaning up this mess." With that, I left my quarters, closing the door on their antics as I went.

Tor was across the hall in his own temporary quarters until we could solidify the deal between the Rhonar and Earth. Now that we had the ergamite, it was only a matter of time.

"My lovely little captain," Tor rose and claimed me in his embrace, "I missed you."

"Cocky commander," I nuzzled his chest, "I wasn't gone that long."

He sat on the bed, bringing me with him. "Thirty clicks is a near eternity."

"Needy warrior." I laughed against his lips as we kissed. His tongue swept inside my mouth and all thoughts flew from my head. When we broke apart, I straddled his waist. He linked our hands together, and I stared at the new markings on his forearms and wrist. "I love your katra." I circled the metallic pattern he'd chosen for me —a series of swirls that glowed in contrast to his skin. "And I love you."

"I love you, Jane." He guided me over his hardened cock, angling my hips as he did. "Let me show you how much." He pulled me down for another long, languorous kiss. *Let me show you forever.*

I smiled, thinking of the lingerie I'd hidden beneath my clothes. I couldn't wait to show him. Now and always. *I think that can be arranged.*

MIACH

"Thank you." I handed the instructions to my assistant, hoping he didn't crex up anything while I signed off for the night. As the primary healer of the Rhonar I took my job seriously, even if I acted like a draving fool half the time. It was the only way I knew to keep the hunger at bay and stop my abilities from dragging me into the void. If I didn't take the universe too seriously, then the universe couldn't crex with me.

That's what I'd believed before the little Terran came into my life.

Rising from my desk, I headed for the gym. My palms were sweating, and I needed a cleanser desperately, but my mind raced with other desires. At this time of night, everyone was thankfully in their quarters or on the night shift. I stripped off my leathers and dove into the water. The battle cruiser was outfitted with everything a warrior required in deep space. As that included exercise, a pool was built into the gym with its own gravitational field. Should the ship be attacked and power lost, the water would remain in place, thanks to the separate circuit of regenerating power.

That's what the stealth shields need. I worked through the problem as I swam. Ever since the tiny blond Terran had sent me the assignment from her captain, I'd been itching to work on it. But with Commander Tor on leave as he bonded with his mate, and the negotiations with Earth continuing, I'd had my hands full on the battle cruiser.

I stopped mid-stroke and spit out a mouthful of water. "That's a crexing lie."

No one needed me. The Versaken had been pushed from Earth's orbit—for now. With the plans for the ergamite to power shields around the Terrans' planet, we'd soon be able to protect them without the constant need for battle. And other than the occasional sick warrior—which Celestia knew was bad enough—with luck the med-wing would be an empty place.

You're avoiding the assignment because of her. I closed my eyes and dunked my head under the water, the cold feel of it lapping at my ears. An image of the beautiful female appeared behind my closed lids. Her honey-yellow hair, fair skin, dark dots across her nose, bright hazel eyes, and plump little body I yearned to feel against mine...I was sunk. *Crex.*

I cut through the pool like a spear sliced the air. Water sloshed everywhere. Hoisting my chest over the side, I climbed out and stomped for the drying unit. The warm rays zapped the moisture from my skin. I dressed and headed for the communications room. Placing a call to the moonbase, I waited for a response.

"Hi Miach!" The source of my torment appeared on the screen. "Did you read my report? Ready to get to work?"

"Greetings, Taylor," I said coolly. I had to squash this hope between us. The hunger gnawed inside me like a ravenous beast, threatening to devour this lovely *sakasha* whole. I'd not be the cause of her downfall. "I reviewed the material. I'm afraid I see no merit in your plan."

Her brows shot toward her nose as her mouth tightened. "Miach, I can tell something is up with you." She plopped her hand under her chin. "You going to tell me about it, or just act like a jerk?'

I bit back a smile. Taylor was the personification of sunshine. Even the coldest ice would be melted by her rays. But I couldn't reveal my problem—*she* was my problem. "It's nothing." I waved it away, hoping to throw her off the scent.

"Uh-huh." She stretched her arms overhead. "Well, usually you're a ton of fun to be around, but since you're being so grumpy," her eyes twinkled with mischief, "you'll have to be punished."

My cock hardened at her words. I inwardly cursed the damn thing. It was a liar. Wanting this female didn't make a future for us. "Specialist, I don't report to you."

"Whoa!" Flapping her hands at the screen, she straightened. "You really *are* in a mood."

"Can we get on with this then?" I ground my teeth. Keeping up this bastard persona toward her was harder than I'd thought it'd be.

"Mr. Alien," she stared pointedly at me, "*you* called *me*." She brushed strands of wayward hair from her face. "In the middle of the night, I might add."

I squeezed my hands into fists under the communications table. "Right."

"Sooo," she elongated the word. "What's the deal, Miach? You going to help me with the stealth shielding, or you going to hide on your cruiser?"

"I'm not hiding." The little female's perception was uncanny. I thought my ability to determine what was wrong with a person if I was in close proximity to them was invasive enough, but this Terran cut right to the heart of a male.

"Sure, sure." She reclined in her chair, hands crossed over her stomach. "Whatever you say."

"Sakasha," I snorted, "I am *not* hiding."

"And there you go with that nickname again." She threw her hands in the air. "Are you ever going to tell me what that means?"

"No," I said with finality.

She huffed. "Fine, be that way. But get your ass over to the moonbase by 0800 hours. Don't be late."

The communique ended.

"Drav it!" That had not gone as planned. I'd pushed the little Terran away, hoping to make her hate me. But every time she returned in full force. It was a crexing curse. No matter how much I wanted her, the hunger beat inside me, revealing the truth.

Taylor was not my mate.

Thank you for reading! Did you enjoy? Please add your review because nothing helps an author more and encourages readers to take a chance on a book than a review.

Want a special **BONUS SCENE** of Tor and Jane doing a little role-play with lingerie? Then join my newsletter HERE for that upcoming bonus release, and all the latest sales, reveals, and giveaways!

And don't miss more in the Earth Brides & Alien Warriors series with book four, ALIEN'S HOPE, coming soon!

Until then check out Alien's Getaway available here or FREE to newsletter subscribers. Turn the page for a sneak peek!

This book has been edited and proofed. However, pesky grammar gremlins are like space dust, you just can't get rid of it! If you would like to help fight the battle against them, however, please feel free to send them to AlienBookLover@gmail.com with the Subject Line: GRAMMAR GREMLINS.

Thank you and happy reading!

Sneak Peek of Alien's Getaway

ELENA

"You know, I swore off helping humans the *last* time I had to pose as a slave." Jadara shook her head, her fire locks dancing with the movement like living flames.

"I know, girl." I crept closer behind her and grabbed her arm. My usual golden brown complexion appeared a shade too pale after months spent on a deep space vessel. It stood in contrast to my alien friend's bright blue shade. I sighed at the thought, aching for planetary ground and sunshine. Lots of sunshine. "I promise once we escape this so-called space cruise, I'll owe you one."

"Some cruise," she muttered. Tugging at the yellow scarves banded around her breasts, she attempted to hide more of her exposed skin for the fifth time. Matching fabric hung from her waist in strategic positions to cover her sensitive areas. Strappy sandals of the same banana hue completed the outfit. "Gah!" Her hands flopped at her sides, giving up on her fidgeting for the time being. "I can't believe I fell for their 'guaranteed pleasure for all' shtick."

"Well, it is a catchy slogan," I offered. She huffed at that, and I didn't remark further. It was on the tip of my tongue to continue with a funny story or a round of sarcasm, but I held back. Comedy was my go-to for tense situations, but years working as a security officer taught me to curb the humor.

We fell into a companionable silence as we waited, hidden behind a hexagonal potted plant three times our size. The burgundy leaves provided the perfect coverage to spy on our captors. That was if Jadara could stay still for more than two minutes. "Elena…" She tapped a pointed nail on her chin and glanced at me. "Where are these eepobars anyway?"

"Eep-oh, what now?" I raised a brow at her.

I'd been lucky to find Jadara and employ her help. After the attack on DS1—the first deep space vessel sent from Earth to create a colony on a new planet—my crew was scattered. With the help of our chief security officer and our ship's doctor, we managed to get some of the science team off the ship safely. They were the most vital of us as they had the knowledge to create the colony. But their escape was a near thing as the bastards had hit us from multiple points, battering the ship. With a little luck, we managed to steer the scientists into an escape capsule and launch it with stealth shielding. It was the best we could do given the circumstances. What happened after that…well, I was still rattled from it.

"Eepobars," Jadara repeated, snapping me back to the present. "Isn't that what you called them?"

"You mean hippo-bears?" I snorted. Our attackers had turned out to be a gang of space thugs, a species called the Mangox. Hell bent on causing havoc, they were apparently the biggest and baddest of all the nasty players in the Meta Sector. Engaging in everything from underground weapons procurement to slave trading, their current con was the SpaceZ Pleasure Cruise. It's where I found myself after they abducted everyone left aboard DS1 that didn't have the luck of escaping. Although, I wouldn't have abandoned ship, even if I'd had the chance. *Never.*

Jadara, as if sensing my distraction, pivoted quietly on her sandaled heel toward me. "Yeah, you said the Mangox were eepobears. It's a curse, no?"

"Not quite." A chuckle bubbled in my chest. "I was saying they looked like a cross between a hippo and a bear, two animals from my home planet."

"Oh." She spun around to continue our watch. "Well, they may look like that, but animals are too good for these monsters. They're nothing but asshats."

The laughter I'd been holding back broke free, and I had to clasp a hand over my mouth to contain it.

"Shhh," she hissed at me. "We're supposed to be stealthy, remember?"

"*I* told *you* that." I flicked at her shoulder to emphasize my point. "You're the one that's throwing around Earth slang like you were born to use it. How am I not supposed to laugh?"

Casting a withering stare over her shoulder, she scoffed. "You'll manage, Miss Security."

"Just keep an eye out. We need to find a way to locate my friends and get off this damn ship." I fussed with my own outfit, a replica of Jadara's except the fabric was purple instead of yellow. *What I wouldn't give for that ugly navy jumpsuit.* My security uniform had been a drab design, but it was functional and comfortable, and oh how I missed it. After the attack, the Mangox had blasted our ship with some type of chemical concoction, knocking us unconscious. We didn't even have the opportunity to fight back. When I'd come to fully for the first time, I awoke in a room filled with tropical plants. Little did I know it was a simulation on this accursed space cruise.

Waiting as we were now had my mind wandering to that nightmare memory that was far too fresh.

"Where am I?" My head throbbed as if I'd gone on a two-day bender. Since I rarely ever drank, and certainly not enough to blackout, that didn't seem plausible. I rose slowly, the acids in my stomach rising with me. Ugh. I put a hand to my chest as if to stem the tide. But with the world around me spinning and my head throbbing, it was a lost battle. I fell onto my hands and knees gagging. Fortunately, or unfortunately, depending on how you viewed it, nothing came up.

"Great. So I'm probably dehydrated too." As if summoning the feeling into existence, I rasped against a dry throat. The pain caused tingles over my neck that had me dreaming of water. It was

only then the dizziness and nauseous eased enough for me to take in my surroundings.

Bright blue plants filled every inch of the space, dotting the pink sand with patches of black soil. With long ashen trunks and wide leaves that gave off a turquoise glow, they reminded me of palm trees. My family had lived in Puerto Rico for generations before the diminishing of viable land on Earth, and although I'd never seen the plants in person, my family had enough holo-vids standing beside them to make me feel as if I had.

Remaining on my hands and knees, I reached for a teal frond that rested near my head. "Soft." I mumbled. My thoughts were sluggish as if moving through pudding. I used the texture of the leaf to help ground me. The leaf crumbled beneath my ministrations, but the action worked to pull me from the chemical-induced fog. I rose fully this time. With my legs under me, wobbling slightly, I managed to stay standing. "What is this place?"

As if in answer, a beam of light hit me. I shielded my eyes, but the strange glow encapsulated me. Then, a disembodied voice spoke. "Come one, come all to the paradise sector! A new treasure for you is on display."

I scanned the skyline where the voice seemed to be speaking from above. I wished I hadn't. Another round of nauseous threatened. Beyond the treetops a clear glass panel encircled what should have been the sky. This was no natural environment. It had been created for observation. And as the white light continued to shine on me, I knew in my heart the truth.

"It's a goddess damned zoo."

I shook my head violently as if to dislodge the memory. It hadn't been long after that I'd found Jadara. Taken from the "paradise" habitat as our captors called it, I was placed in a barred cell at night. My blue alien friend had apparently complained after seeing what the pleasure cruise actually was—a glorified slave market—and had been taken into custody for her outbursts by the ship's security. Housed in the same cell as me, she explained everything about the Mangox and their scam, which she had learned of the hard way.

"All I wanted was a nice, relaxing vacation," she'd said to me the first night of our captivity together. "Okay, and maybe a little fling too. Is that too much to ask for?"

I'd commiserated, having wanted a new life among the stars as opposed to being planet-bound on ever decreasing Earth's land masses. And okay, yeah, a galactic romance might have been on my mind too. But neither of us got what we wanted. Instead of her dream vacation, she'd been horrified to learn she'd ended up on a slaver's ship masquerading as a space cruise. And well, Jadara, being a fierce rebel as I soon discovered, wasn't one to keep quiet or back down when faced with injustice.

Lucky for me.

So here we were. Broken free of our captivity—thanks to my cousin Antonio's insistence that thievery was a valiant and noble tradition, and therefore, teaching me all about electro lock-picking as a child. I never thought I'd have to use the specific skill in space, but I wasn't complaining. Now, we had to discover what happened to the rest of my crew.

I shifted closer to Jadara so we crouched side by side, observing our captors.

"Did you show the bastards to the display windows?" The obvious leader of the Mangox trio glared at his subordinates. Standing at what had to be at least eight feet tall, his thick hind legs rivaled the tree trunks in the paradise habitat. The Mangox might walk on two legs, but their arms were equally as beefy, hinting at a quadruped ancestry. Although the two underlings were not quite as large as their boss, they still towered above Jadara and me.

"Yes, Capo Gorox," the pair answered in unison and snapped to attention. Their backs straightened, thrusting their bear-like chests forward. Woolly brown fur covered every inch of their visible bodies, which was considerable since they wore only beige button-down uniform shirts, belts that housed weapons instead of holding up pants, and glistening golden helmets with horns. The lack of pants or footwear made their appearance all the more savage.

"Good." The one they called Gorox waved toward a door across the hall. "They've had ample time to look then. Bring them here and let's have their selection." He snorted, the motion vibrating along his snout. Too thin and short to be an elephant's trunk, it reminded me a little of a tapir. "If none suit their liking, we will bring more from the cells."

I stiffened at that.

"If they check the cells," Jadara whispered in my ear.

"I know." A cold dread raised goosebumps along my skin. We were running out of time. The Mangox hadn't learned of our escape yet. Picking the electro lock and freeing ourselves had been a strategic move. We waited weeks before enacting our plan so we'd learn the schedule set for us, the guard rotations, everything. Now, one freak unanticipated cell check could ruin it all.

Jadara fidgeted beside me. I rested a staying hand on her arm. "Just wait." We had no other choice. If we didn't stick to the plan, we were toast. "It'll be okay."

I didn't know if she believed that, but she didn't get a chance to reply. The hallway door opened and out walked the most incredible creature I'd ever seen. Almost as tall as the Mangox, the male had a broad chest covered by two bronzed shoulder pieces, thick straps, and nothing else. The straps served as a harness for the wicked looking weapon peaking from above his back. Black leather-like pants and boots covered his long legs and feet. Straight black hair streaked with silver was tied by a piece of cloth at the nape of his neck. Two dark brows rested atop amber-hued eyes with black pupils that held flames. It was like staring into a roaring fire. His jaw was sharper than diamonds but his lips were lush. He had a humanoid face, but with just enough differences to be truly… "Alien."

"Duh." Another of Earth's slang passed Jadara's lips while she rolled her eyes at me as if I'd lost my mind. "But we're in luck. That's a Rhonar warrior."

"An alien warrior?" I gulped. Yeah, he looked like one all right, a come-to-life barbarian ripped from the classic sci-fi romance novels. I mean not that I hoarded my collection of holo-books with back-ups on multiple sky drives or anything. Nope, not me. *Righhht.*

"Yes." She leaned forward through the burgundy leaves for a better view, and I followed her actions. "I met up with them on Craxon, the planet I told you about where I was part of the rebellion."

As if I could forget her starting a planetary wide uprising where she'd found one of the missing Earth scientists from DS1. My captain and fellow officers had fought so hard to help as many as we could escape, but I knew some were left behind. I only hoped anyone taken had been transported to the same place as me. Unfortunately, the cosmic fates didn't like me that much. Still some *had* to be here. *I'll find them.*

"Officer Rivera, are you listening?" She used my title, which she knew annoyed me, and tapped my shoulder.

I sucked on the side of my cheek. Clearly, I'd been in space too long if I was sizing up this hunky ass alien like a dessert buffet. "Yeah, I'm listening."

I wasn't.

The alien warrior sniffed the air, inclining his head in our direction. We both jumped back, not wanting even a potential friendly face to spot us with the Mangox so close. He narrowed his eyes before turning to the sleazy Gorox. "As I said before, I'm searching for a particular…" He paused and his nostrils flared as if he could smell us, which I had no idea if he could or not. "Variety."

"You mentioned having singular tastes." Gorox bent at the waist but not fully. It was a strange half-bow as if trying to placate his customer. "We serve all types of delicacies. Our range is eclectic and our quality top tier."

"So I've been told." The alien warrior crossed his arms over that ample chest, showing off biceps and shoulders that housed unique tattoos. I crept a teeny bit closer through the burgundy plant for a better view. The markings had the appearance of tribal designs but instead of ink, it flowed like metal branded to his skin.

"Yes, well," the Mangox motioned for his subordinates to step closer, "I'm sure we can accommodate your needs." One of the two underlings handed Gorox a type of holo-pad. "You're the only Rhonar visiting the SpaceZ Pleasure Cruise this trip, is that correct?"

"And what business is that of yours?" The warrior growled and his body seemed to swell larger at the sound.

Gorox waved off the question with one beefy furred hand. "None at all. We simply like to make sure we have the ship's manifest correct." A smarmy smile stretched under his snout giving him a cartoonish visage. "Wouldn't want any stowaways. Right, Sir…"

The alien pinched the bridge of his nose, a humanoid gesture that had me silently analyzing our similar looks and wondering at the possibilities. "Daegan," the warrior said, and pointed at the holo-pad. "Just Daegan."

I sucked in a breath at the reveal of his name. Something coiled inside me as if I'd discovered a secret that had to be kept safe. But I didn't have long to ponder my reaction as he continued speaking to the Mangox.

"I'm the solo Rhonar warrior on this ship you have the balls to call a pleasure cruise." His fingers scratched at his shoulder, dangerously close to the handle of his weapon. "Now, do you have what I need or am I wasting my time?"

The Mangox capo stamped his feet and scanned the holo-pad. "Let's see here. You filled out our questionnaire and viewed our display cases. It seems you were looking for a female from…" Gorox turned to the lackey that had handed him the device. "What's this planet again?"

Daegan knocked the holo-pad to the side, forcing Gorox to spin with the movement. At the same time, he drew the weapon—a spiked axe—from his back and held the sharpened and bladed edge against the Mangox's throat. The axe had to have been as long as my arm and forged from glistening golden metal. It had spikes on the flat part of the blade that appeared as sharp its edge. The streaming hallway lights brightened the weapon so it shone with a lethal gleam.

I gripped Jadara's forearm hard. A sense of foreboding tightened my gut.

"I am looking for a Terran." Daegan growled into the face of the beady-eyed capo. "And the planet they're from is Earth."

♄

Don't stop now. Keep reading with your copy of Alien's Getaway available here or FREE to newsletter subscribers.

And if you'd like to connect about the Earth Brides & Alien Warriors series with other readers, I'd love to have you join my Reader Group.

Want even more behind-the-scenes access with exclusive content, spicy art, steamy scenes, special discounts, and more? Check out my Patreon for all the details.

Don't miss book four, ALIEN'S HOPE, coming soon, and discover more from Tina Moss at www.tinamoss.com

Until then, read ALIEN'S GETAWAY, the novella story set to launch the next series, *Lost Brides and Alien Warriors*!

♄

As a security officer of Earth's first deep space vessel, I always believed there were aliens in outer space. I didn't imagine they'd be total jerks.

I might not have bought a ticket for the SpaceZ Pleasure Cruise, yet here I am, brought aboard as the… entertainment. Abducted and far from home, I must rely on new alien allies to escape my captors.

A sexy Rhonar warrior might be the biggest wild card of them all. When our enemies set off the self-destructive sequence, we're thrown into an escape pod together. Crash-landing on a distant planet was not part of the getaway plan.

Alone with the big lug, he's soon calling me his fated mate. Too bad I'm not the romantic kind. Yet, as we fight for each other's survival I can't help but being drawn to his inner fire. And well, his outside is smoking hot too.

Will we be able to find a path free of the planet's twisted caverns? And do I dare trust in the cosmic bond pulling us together?

Only the stars know.

Alien's Getaway is a sci-fi romance and the prequel of the Lost Brides and Alien Warriors series, but it can be read as a standalone. Will they find their brides? Steamy seduction, fated mates, and a happily-ever-after guaranteed.

Acknowledgments

One day I'm going to stop this rapid writing pace, but today is not that day. And while I sink into another caffeine-induced writing session that will inevitably keep me up until the wee hours of the morning, I may be writing solo, but I am never alone. Thank you to all who travel this road with me.

To my hubs, who peppers me with questions like, "When are you stopping for the evening?" and "Do you really need to take the laptop?" The answers are always the same, "I don't know," and "Yes." But points for you for asking them anyway. Perhaps, one day the answers will be different. Perhaps. Thank you for letting me kick you out of the house and for putting my with late night marathon writing sessions. You are my alien, always.

To all my family and friends, who grow by the day. I am so fortunate that you understand (or at least pretend to) this wild thing called being a writer. Thanks for your endless support, boundless enthusiasm, and infinite humor. And yes, Wayne, I'm quite good at world-building. I know that's why you read my books. **wink**

To my Patrons and Reader Group lovelies, I still think we need a cool team name. Spores? Sprouts? I am Moss after all. But regardless, thank you for taking the journey with me and supporting my process. Whether it's posting at 3am with the inevitable, "Do you like this or this better?" question, or sharing ridiculous TikToks, you are there with gusto. Thank you!

To Vivi and Becka, my darlings, I cannot thank you enough. You shine such a light on social media with your thoughtful reviews and infinite love of books. I am so grateful to have you as readers. You are simply the best. Much love.

And last, but always first, to my readers. You are more important than you know, more powerful than you believe, and more deserving than you think. Thank you for reading these spicy alien books! I hope they put a smile on your face and encourage you to remember that you are worthy of everything you desire. I adore you! Until the stars align, and we meet again!

About the Author

TINA MOSS s a USA Today Bestselling Author of urban fantasy, paranormal romance, and sci-fi romance. She lives in NYC with a supportive husband and corgi Bear, though both the males hog the bed and refuse to share the covers. Her corgi Chuck now lives in her heart. When not writing, she enjoys reading, watching cheesy horror flicks, and traveling. As a 5'1″ Shotokan black belt, she firmly believes that fierce things come in small packages.

www.tinamoss.com